FROM THE BOOKS OF

Jane Wilson

Under the tree was a grassy mound. On this
Elaine was invited to sit.
(*Marjorie Dean, College Junior*)   *Page 66*

MARJORIE DEAN
COLLEGE JUNIOR

By PAULINE LESTER

Author of

"Marjorie Dean, College Freshman," "Marjorie Dean, College Sophomore," "Marjorie Dean, College Senior," *and* *The Marjorie Dean High School Series*

A. L. BURT COMPANY
Publishers   New York

THE
Marjorie Dean College Series

A Series of Stories for Girls 12 to 18 Years of Age

By PAULINE LESTER

Marjorie Dean, College Freshman
Marjorie Dean, College Sophomore
Marjorie Dean, College Junior
Marjorie Dean, College Senior

MARJORIE DEAN, COLLEGE JUNIOR.

CHAPTER I

A MUSICAL WELCOME

"REMEMBER; we are to begin with the 'Serenata.' Follow that with 'How Fair Art Thou' and 'Hymn to Hamilton.' Just as we are leaving, sing 'How Can I Leave Thee, Dear?' We will fade away on the last of that. Want to make any changes in the programme?"

Phyllis Moore turned inquiringly to her choristers. There were seven of them including herself, and they were preparing to serenade Marjorie Dean and her four chums. The Lookouts had returned to Hamilton College that afternoon from the long summer vacation. This year, their Silverton Hall friends had arrived before them. Hence Phyllis's plan to serenade them.

Robina Page, Portia Graham, Blanche Scott,

Elaine Hunter, Marie Peyton and Marie's freshman cousin, Hope Morris, comprised Phyllis's serenading party. The latter had been invited to par-
ticipate because she was still company. Incident-
ally she knew the songs chosen, with the exception
of the "Hymn to Hamilton," and could sing alto.
She was, therefore, a valuable asset.

"I hope Leila has managed to cage the girls in
Marjorie's room," remarked Blanche Scott. "We
want all five Sanfordites in on the serenade."

"Leave it to Irish Leila to cage anything she
starts out to cage," was Robin's confident assurance. "If she says she will do a thing, she will
accomplish it, somehow. Leila is a diplomat, and
so clever she is amazing."

"Vera Mason isn't far behind her. Those two
have chummed together so long their methods are
similar. They were the first girls I knew at Hamilton. They met the train I came in on. Nella Sherman and Selma Sanbourne were with them. Two
more fine girls. Portia looked pleasantly reminiscent of her reception by the quartette to which she
now referred.

"I heard Selma Sanbourne wasn't coming back.
I must ask Leila about that." Robin made mental
note of the question.

"That will be hard on Nella," observed Elaine

Hunter, with her usual ready sympathy. "They have always been such great chums."

"Sorry to interrupt, but we must be hiking, girls." In command of the tuneful expedition, Phyllis tucked her violin case under her arm in business-like fashion and cast a critical eye over her flock.

"Be sure you have your instruments of torture with you," she laughed. "One time, at home, three girls and myself started out to serenade a friend of ours. Before we started we had all been sitting on our veranda, eating ice cream. One of the girls was to accompany us on the mandolin. She walked away and left it on the veranda. She never noticed the omission until we were ready to lift up our voices. So we had to sing without it, for it was over a mile to our house and she couldn't very well go back after it."

"Let this be a warning to you mandolin players not to do likewise." Marie turned a severe eye on Elaine and Portia, who made pretext of clutching their mandolins in a firmer grip.

"My good old guitar is hung to me by a ribbon. I am not likely to go away from here without it." Blanche patted the smooth, shining back of the guitar.

"We couldn't have chosen a better time for a serenade," exulted Robin. "It is a fine night; just dark enough. Besides, there are not many girls back at Wayland Hall yet. We won't be so conspicuous with our caroling."

Meanwhile, in a certain room at Wayland Hall, wily Lelia Harper was exerting herself to be agreeable to her Lookout chums. Three of them she had marshalled to Marjorie's room on plea of showing them souvenirs of a trip she had made through Ireland that summer.

The souvenirs had been heartily admired, but even they could not stem Muriel's and Jerry's determined desire to entertain. First Jerry innocently proposed that they all walk over to Baretti's for ices. Leila and Vera exhibited no enthusiasm at the invitation. Next, Muriel re-proposed the jaunt at her expense. Vera cast an appealing look toward Leila. The latter was equal to the occasion.

"And are you so tired of me and my pictures of my Emerald Isle that you want to hurry me off to Baretti's to be rid of me?" she questioned, in an offended tone.

"Certainly not, and you needn't pretend you think so, for you don't," retorted Muriel, unabashed. "Your Irish views are wonderful. So is Baretti's fresh peach ice cream. Helen was there and had some this afternoon. She said it was better than ever. I was only trying to be hospitable and so was Jerry. Sorry you had to take me too personally."

Muriel now strove to simulate offense. She turned up her nose, tossed her head and burst out laughing. "It's no use," she said, "I couldn't really fuss with you if I tried, Leila Greatheart."

"I am relieved to hear it," Leila returned with inimitable dryness.

"Lots of time for Baretti's and ice cream yet tonight. It's only half-past eight." Marjorie indicated the wall clock with a slight move of her head. "We can leave here about nine. We'll be there by ten after."

"Certainly; we have oceans of time," Leila agreed with alacrity. "The ten-thirty rule is still on a vacation and won't be back for a week or so."

"Oh, I haven't told you about my new car," Vera began with sudden inspiration. "Father bought it for me in August. It is a beauty. He is going to send James, his chauffeur, here with it. It may arrive tomorrow. I hope it does." Vera launched into a description of her car with intent to kill time. Phyllis had set the hour for the serenade to the Lookouts at a quarter to nine.

"It will be good and dark then," she had told Leila and Vera. "We will have to come as early as that, for we are going to Acasia House to serenade Barbara Severn, and to Alston Terrace to sing to Isabel Keller. Last, we are going to serenade Miss Humphrey. We'll have to hustle, in order to

go the rounds and get back to Silverton Hall before
eleven o'clock. I depend on you, Leila, to keep that
lively bunch of Sandfordites in until we get there."

Leila, aided by Vera, was now endeavoring to
carry out Phyllis's request. She was privately hoping that the serenaders would be on time. Should
they delay until nine or after, they were quite likely
to gather in under the window of a deserted room.

Readers of the "MARJORIE DEAN HIGH SCHOOL
SERIES" have long been in touch with Marjorie
Dean and the friends of her high school days.
"MARJORIE DEAN, HIGH SCHOOL FRESHMAN," re-
counted her advent into Sanford High School and
what happened to her during her first year there.
"MARJORIE DEAN, HIGH SCHOOL SOPHOMORE,"
"MARJORIE DEAN, HIGH SCHOOL JUNIOR," and
"MARJORIE DEAN, HIGH SCHOOL SENIOR," com-
pleted a series of stories which dealt entirely with
Marjorie's four years' course at Sanford High
School. Admirers of the loyal-hearted, high-prin-
cipled young girl, who became a power at high
school because of her many fine qualities, will recall
her ardent wish to enroll as a student at Hamilton
College when she should have finished her high
school days.

In "MARJORIE DEAN, COLLEGE FRESHMAN,"
will be found the account of Marjorie's doings as a
freshman at Hamilton College. Entering college

full of noble resolves and high ideals, she was not disappointed in her Alma Mater, although she was not long in discovering that an element of snobbery was abroad at Hamilton which was totally against Hamilton traditions. Aided by four of her Sanford chums, who had entered Hamilton College with her, and a number of freshmen and upper class girls, of democratic mind, the energetic band had endeavored to combat the pernicious influence, exercised by a clique of moneyed girls, which was fast taking hold upon other students. The end of the college year had found their efforts successful, in a measure, and the way paved for better things.

In "MARJORIE DEAN, COLLEGE SOPHOMORE," the further account of Marjorie's eventful college days was set forth. Opposed, from her return to Hamilton College by certain girls residing in the same house with herself, who disliked her independence and fair-mindedness, Marjorie was later given signal proof of their enmity. How she and her chums fought them on their own ground and won a notable victory over them formed a narrative of pleasing interest and lively action.

Now that the Five Travelers, as the quintette of Sanford girls loved to call themselves, were once more settled in the country of college, their devoted friends had already planned to honor them. Leila and Vera, who invariably returned early to college, had encountered Phyllis on the campus on the day previous. Informing her of the Lookouts' expected arrival on the next afternoon, Phyllis had planned the serenade and demanded Leila's help. Leila had rashly promised to keep the arrivals at home that evening. She was now of the opinion that a promise was sometimes easier made than fulfilled.

"Since Vera has told you everything she can remember about her new roadster, I shall now do a little talking myself." Leila was having the utmost difficulty in controlling her risibles. She dared not look at Vera; nor dared Vera look at her. "Ahem! When I was in Ireland," she pompously announced, "I saw——"

Came the welcome interruption for which she had been waiting. Clear and sweet under the windows of the room rose the strains of Tosti's "Serenata." A brief prelude and voices took it up, filling the evening air with harmony.

"Thank my stars! A-h-h!" Leila relaxed exaggeratedly in her chair, her Cheshire-cat smile predominating her features.

"You bad old rascal!" Marjorie paused long enough to shake Leila playfully by the shoulders. Then she hurried to one of the windows. Jerry, Muriel and Lucy had reached one. Ronny and Vera were at the other. Marjorie joined them.

Leila made no move to rise.   She preferred sitting where she was.

"Keep quiet," Jerry had admonished at the first sounds.   "If we start to talk to them, they'll stop singing.   Whoever they are, they certainly can sing. Her companions of her mind, it was a silent and appreciative little audience that gathered at the open windows to listen to the serenaders.

There was no moon that night.   It was impossible to see the faces of the carolers, nor, in the general harmony of melodious sound, was it possible to identify any one voice.   An energetic clapping of hands, from other windows as well as those of Marjorie's room, greeted the close of the "Serenata."   Then a high soprano voice, which the girls recognized as Robin Page's, began that most beautiful of old songs, "How Fair Art Thou."   A violin throbbed a soft obligato.

The marked hush that hung over the Hall during the rendering of the song was most complimentary to the soloist.   The serenaders were not out for glory, however.   Hardly had the applause accorded Robin died out, when mandolins, guitar and violin took up the stately "Hymn to Hamilton."

"First in wisdom, first in precept; teach us to revere
     thy way:

Grant us mind to know thy purpose, keep us in
    thy brightest ray.
Let our acts be shaped in honor; let our steps be
    just and free:
Make us worthy of thy threshold, as we pledge our
    faith to thee."

Thus ran the first stanza, set to a sonorous air
which the combined harmony of voices and musical
instruments rendered doubly beautiful. It seemed
to those honored by the seranaders that they had
never before heard the fine old hymn so inspiringly
sung. The whole three stanzas were given. The
instant the hymn was ended the familiar melody
"How Can I Leave Thee Dear?" followed.

"That means they are going to beat it," called
Jerry in low tones. "Let us head them off before
they can get away and take them with us to
Baretti's. We'll have to start now, if we expect to
catch them. They're beginning the second stanza.
We'll just give *them* a little surprise."

With one accord the appreciative and mischievous audience left the windows and made a rush for
the stairs. Headed by Jerry they exited quietly
from the house and stole around its right-hand
corner.

Absorbed in their own lyric efforts, the singers
had reached the third sentimentally pathetic stanza:

"If but a bird were I, homeward to thee I'd fly;
  Falcon nor hawk I'd fear, if thou wert near.
  Shot by a hunter's ball; would at thy feet I fall,
  If but one ling'ring tear would dim thine eye."

Ready to leave almost on the last line, they were
not prepared for the merry crowd of girls who
pounced suddenly upon them.

"How can you leave us, dears?" caroled Muriel
Harding, as she caught firm hold of Robin Page.
"You are not going to leave us. Don't imagine it
for a minute."

CHAPTER II

UNDER THE SEPTEMBER STARS

"Captured by Sanfordites!" exclaimed Robin
dramatically. "What fate is left to us now?" Despite her tragic utterance, she proceeded to a vigorous hand-shaking with Muriel.

"Now why couldn't you have stayed upstairs like
nice children and praised our modest efforts in your
behalf instead of prancing down stairs to head us
off?" inquired Phyllis in pretended disgust. "Not
one of you has the proper idea of the romance which
should attend a serenade. Of course, you didn't

know who was singing to you, and, of course, you just simply *had* to find out."

"Don't delude yourself with any such wild idea," Jerry made haste to retort. "We knew Robin's voice the minute she opened her mouth to sing 'How Fair Art Thou.' Now which one of us were you particularly referring to in that number? I took it straight to myself. Of course I *may* be a trifle presumptuous, Ahem!"

"Yes; 'Ahem!'" mimicked Phyllis. "You are just the same good old, funny old scout, Jeremiah. Somebody please hold my violin while I embrace Jeremiah."

"Hold it yourself," laughed Portia. "We have fond welcomes of our own to hand around and need the use of our arms."

Full of the happiness of the meeting the running treble of girlhood, mingled with ripples of gay, light laughter, was music in itself.

"The Moore Symphony Orchestra and Concert Company will have to be moving on," Elaine reminded after fifteen minutes had winged away. "This is Phil's organization but she seems to have forgotten all about it. We are supposed to serenade Barbara Severn, Isabel Keller and Miss Humphrey while the night is yet young. I can see where someone of the trio will have to be unserenaded this evening."

"Couldn't you serenade them tomorrow night?" coaxed Marjorie. "We had it all planned to go to Baretti's before we hustled down to head you off. The instant I recognized Robin's heavenly soprano I knew that the Silvertonites were under our windows. I guess the rest knew, too. We didn't want to talk while you were singing."

"Very polite in you, I am sure." In the darkness Elaine essayed a profound bow. Result, her head came into smart contact with Blanche's guitar.

"Steady there! I need my guitar for the next orchestral spasm." Blanche swung the instrument under her arm out of harm's way.

"I need my head, too," giggled Elaine, ruefully rubbing that slightly injured member.

"Do serenade the others tomorrow night." Ronny now added her plea. "How would you like to take us along with you, then? Not to sing, but just for company, you know. I never went out serenading, and I fully feel the need of excitement."

"What you folks need is fresh peach ice cream and lots of it," Jerry advised with crafty enthusiasm. It's to be had at Guiseppe Baretti's."

"I know of nothing more refreshing to tired soloists than fresh peach ice cream," seconded Vera. "I leave it to my esteemed friend, Irish Leila, if I am not entirely correct in this."

"You are. Now what is it that you are quite

right about?" Leila had caught the last sentence and risen to the occasion.

"Such support," murmured Vera, as a laugh arose.

"Is it not now?" Leila blandly commented. "Never worry. There is little I would not agree with you in, Midget. Be consoled with that handsome amend. As for you singers and wandering musicians, you had better come with us.

"We'll feed you on fine white bread of the wheat
    And the drip of honey gold:
We'll give you pale clouds for a mantle sweet,
    And a handful of stars to hold."

Leila sang lightly the quaint words of an old Irish ditty.

"Can we resist such a prospect?" laughed Phyllis. "How about it, girls? Is it on with the serenade or on to Baretti's?"

"Baretti's it had better be, since we are invited there by such distinguished persons," was Robin's decision. "Leila, you are to teach me that song you were just humming. It is sweet!"

Her companions were nothing loath to abandon their project for the evening in order to hob-nob with their Wayland Hall friends. They came to this decision very summarily. Now fourteen strong, the company turned their steps toward their favorite restaurant.

They were nearing the cluster lights stationed at each side of the wide walk leading up to the entrance of the tea room, when Lucy Warner stopped short with: "Oh, girls; I know something that I think would be nice to do."

"Speak up, respected Luciferous," encouraged Vera. "You say so little it is a pleasure to listen to you. I wish I co ld say that of everyone I know," she added significantly.

"Have you an idea of whom she may be talking about?" quizzed Leila, rolling her eyes at her companions.

"She certainly doesn't mean us, even if she didn't say 'present company excepted.' Muriel beamed at Leila with trustful innocence. "Go ahead, Luciferous Warniferous, noble Sanfordite, and tell us what's on your mind."

"I had no idea I was so greatly respected in this crowd. I never before saw signs of it. Much obliged. This is what I thought of." Lucy came to the point with her usual celerity. "Why not serenade Signor Baretti? He is an Italian. The Italians all love music. I know he would like it. You girls sing and play so beautifully."

"Of course he would." Marjorie was the first to endorse Lucy's proposal "This is really a fine time for it, too. It's late enough in the evening so that there won't be many persons in the restaurant."

"It would delight his little, old Guiseppeship," approved Blanche.

"No doubt about it," Robin heartily concurred. "We ought to sing something from an Italian opera. That would please him most. The Latins don't quite understand the beauty of our English and American songs."

"We can sing the sextette from 'Lucia,' " proposed Elaine. "It doesn't matter about the words. We know the music. We have sung that together so many times we wouldn't make a fizzle of it."

"Yes, and there is the 'Italian Song at Nightfall' that Robin sings so wonderfully. We can help out on the last part of it." Tucking her violin under her chin, Phyllis played a few bars of the selection she had named. "I can play it," she nodded. "I never tried it on the fiddle before."

"That's two," counted Robin. "For a third and last let's give that pretty 'Gondelier's Love Song,' by Nevin. It doesn't matter about words to that, either. There aren't any. People ought to learn to appreciate songs without words. Guiseppe won't care a hang about anything but the music. If any of you Wayland Hallites decide to sing with us, sing nicely. Don't you dare make the tiniest discord."

"She has some opinion of herself as a singer," Leila told the others, with comically raised brows. "Be easy. We have no wish to lilt wid yez."

Having decided to serenade the unsuspecting proprietor of the tea room, the next point to be settled was where they should stand to sing.

"Wait a minute. I'll go and look in one of the windows," volunteered Ronny. "Perhaps I shall be able to see just where he is."

"He is usually at his desk about this time in the evening. We'll gather around the window nearest where he is sitting," planned Phyllis.

Ronny flitted lightly ahead of her companions, stopping at a window on the right-hand side, well to the rear. The others followed her more slowly in order to give her time to make the observation. Before they reached her she turned from her post and came quickly to them.

"He is back at the last table on the left reading a newspaper. There isn't a soul in the room but himself," she said in an undertone. "The time couldn't be more opportune."

"Oh, fine," whispered Robin. "We can go around behind the inn and be right at the window nearest him."

"The non-singers, I suppose we might call ourselves the trailers, will politely station our magnificent selves at the next window above the singers to see how the victim takes it," decided Jerry. "Contrary, 'no.' I don't hear any opposing voices."

"There mustn't be *any* voices heard for the next two minutes," warned Portia Graham. "Slide around the inn and take your places as quietly as mice."

In gleeful silence the girls divided into two groups, each group taking up its separate station.

"I hope the night air hasn't played havoc with my strings," breathed Phyllis. "I don't dare try them. Are we ready?" She rapped softly on the face of her violin with the bow.

Followed the tense instant that always precedes the performance of an orchestra, then Phyllis and Robin began the world-known sextette from "Lucia." Robin had sung it so many times in private to the accompaniment of her cousin's violin that the attack was perfect. The others took it up immediately, filling the night with echoing sweetness.

From their position at the next window the watchers saw the dark, solemn face of the Italian raised in bewildered amazement from his paper. Not quite comprehending at first the unbidden flood of music which met his ears, he listened for a moment in patent stupefaction. Soon a smile began to play about his tight little mouth. It widened into a grin of positive pleasure. Guiseppe understood that a great honor was being done him.

He was not only being serenaded, but he was listening to the music of his native country as well.

His varying facial expressions, as the sextette rose and fell, showed his love of the selection. As it ended, he did an odd thing. He rose from his chair, bowed his profound thanks toward the window from whence came the singing, and sat down again, looking expectant.

"He knows very well he's being watched," whispered Marjorie. "Doesn't he look pleased? I'm so glad you thought of him, Lucy."

Lucy was also showing shy satisfaction at the success of her proposal. She was secretly more proud of some small triumph of the kind on her part than of her brilliancy as a student.

Had Signor Baretti been attending a performance of grand opera, he could not have shown a more evident pleasure in the programme. He listened to the entertainment so unexpectedly provided him with the rapt air of a true music-lover.

"There!" softly exclaimed Phyllis, as she lowered her violin. "That's the end of the programme, Signor Baretti. Now for that fresh peach ice cream. I shall have coffee and mountain cake with it. I am as hungry as the average wandering minstrel."

"Let's walk in as calmly as though we had never thought of serenading Guiseppe," said Robin. "Oh, we can't. I forgot. The orchestra part of this aggregation is a dead give-away."

"We don't care. He will know it was we who were out there. There is no one else about but us. I hope he won't think we are a set of little Tommy Tuckers singing for our suppers. That's a horrible afterthought on my part," Elaine laughed.

"Come on." Jerry and her group had now joined the singers. "He saw us but not until you were singing that Nevin selection. He kept staring at the window where the sound came from. We had our faces right close to our window and all of a sudden he looked straight at us. You should have seen him laugh. His whole face broke into funny little smiles."

"He may have thought we were the warblers," suggested Muriel hopefully. "We can parade into the inn on your glory. If I put on airs he may take me for the high soprano." She glanced teasingly at Robin.

"Oh, go as far as you like. It won't be the first instance in the world's history where some have done all the work and others have taken all the credit," Robin reminded.

In this jesting frame of mind the entire party strolled around to the inn's main entrance. At the door they found Guiseppe waiting for them, his dark features wreathed in smiles.

"I wait for you here," he announced, with an eloquent gesture of the hand. "So I know som' my friendly young ladies from the college sing just for me. You come in. You are my com'ny. You say what you like. I give the best. Not since I come this country I hear the singing I like so much. The Lucia! Ah, that is the one I lov'!

"I tell you the little story while you stan' here. Then you come in. When I come this country, I am the very poor boy. Come in the steerage. No much to eat. I fin' work. Then the times hard, I lose work. All over New York I walk, but don't fin'. I have *no one cent*. I am put from the bed I rent. I can no pay. For four days I have the nothing eat. I say, 'It is over.' I am this, that I will walk to the river in the night an' be no more.

"It is the very warm night and I am tired. I walk an' walk." His face took on a shade of his by-gone hopelessness as he continued. "Soon I come the river, I think. Then I hear the music. It is in the next street jus' I go turn into. It is the harp an' violin. Two my countrymen play the Lucia. I am so sad. I sit on a step an' cry. Pretty soon one these ask the money gif' for the music. He touch me on shoulder, say very kind in Italian, *Che c'è mai?* That mean, 'What the matter?' He see I am the Italiano. We look each other. Both cry, then embrac'. He is my oldes' brother. He come here long before me. My mother an' I, we don't hear five years. Then my mother die. Two my brothers work in the *vigna* for the rich *vignaiuolo* in my country. My father is dead long time. So I come here.

"My brother give me the eat, the clothes, the place sleep. He have good room. He work in the day for rich Italian importer. Sometimes he go out play at night for help his friend who play the harp. He is the old man an' don't work all the time. So it is I lov' the Lucia. They don't play that, mebbe I don't sit on that step. Then never fin' my brother. An' you have please me more than for many years you play the Lucia for me this night."

CHAPTER III

A VERANDA ENCOUNTER

It lacked but a few minutes of eleven o'clock when the serenading party said goodnight to Signor Baretti and trooped off toward the campus. The usually taciturn Italian had surprised and touched them by the impulsive story of his most tragic hour. He had afterward played host to his light-hearted guests with the true grace of the

Latin. No one came to the inn for cheer after they
entered in that evening, so they had the place quite
to themselves. After a feast of the coveted peach
ice cream and cakes, the obliging orchestra tuned
up again at Guiseppe's earnest request. Robin sang
Shubert's "Serenade" and "Appear Love at Thy
Window." Phyllis played Raff's "Cavatina" and
one of Brahm's "Hungarian Dances." Blanche
Scott sang "Asleep in the Deep," simply to prove
she had a masculine voice when she chose to use it.

"We'll come and make music for you again
sometime," promised kind-hearted Phyllis as they
left their beaming host.

"I thank you. An' you forget you say you come
an' play, I tell you 'bout it sometime you come here
to eat," he warned the party as they were leaving.

"Talk about truth being stranger than fiction,
what do you think of Guiseppe's story?" Jerry exclaimed as soon as they were well away from the
inn. "Imagine how one would feel to meet one's
long-lost brother just as one was getting ready to
commit suicide!"

"One half of the world doesn't know how the
other half lives," Ronny said with a shake of her
fair head.

"To see Guiseppe today, successful and well-to-
do, one finds it hard to visualize him as the poor,

starved, despondent Italian boy who cried his heart out on the doorstep." Vera's tones vibrated with sympathy. The Italian's story had impressed her deeply.

The girls discussed it soberly as they wended a leisurely way across the campus. Even care-free Muriel, who seldom liked to take life seriously, remarked with becoming earnestness that it was such stories which made one realize one's own benefits.

"Be on hand tomorrow night at eight-thirty sharp," was Phyllis's parting injunction to the Wayland Hall girls as the Silvertonites left them to go on to their own house. "We have three fair ladies to sing to and we don't want to slight any of them."

"I think we ought to get up some entertainments of our own this year. I never stopped to realize before how few clubs and college societies Hamilton has. There's only the 'Silver Pen',—one has to have high literary ability to make that,—the 'Twelfth Night Club' and the 'Fortnightly Debating Society.' We haven't a single sorority," Vera declared with regret.

"Miss Remson told me once of a sorority that Hamilton used to have called the 'Round Table.' It flourished for many years. Then all of a sudden she heard no more of it. She said Hamilton was very different even ten years ago from now. There was little automobiling and more sociability among the campus houses. There were house plays going on every week and different kinds of entertainments in which almost everyone joined."

"That's the way college ought to be," commended Vera. "Even if Hamilton hasn't yet won back to those palmy days, we had more fellowship here last year than the year before. Why, during Leila's and my freshman year here we were seldom invited anywhere. We hardly knew Helen Trent until late in the year. Nella and Selma, Martha Merrick and Rosalind Black were our only friends."

"And now we are to lose Selma." Leila heaved an audible sigh. She had already informed the girls of Selma's approaching marriage to a young naval officer.

"Did Selma know last year she was not going to finish college?" asked Muriel. "If I had gone through three years of my college course I wouldn't give up the last and most important year just to be married."

"That is because you know nothing about love," teased Ronny.

"Do you?" challenged Muriel.

"I do not. I have a good deal more sentiment than you have though," retorted Ronny. "I can appreciate Selma's sacrifice at the shrine of love."

"So could I if I knew more about it," Muriel flung back.

"Precisely what I said to you. So glad you agree with me," chuckled Ronny.

"I don't agree with you at all. I meant if I knew more about what you were pleased to call 'Selma's sacrifice,' not *love*." Muriel's emphasis of the last word proclaimed her disdain of the tender passion.

"Hear the geese converse," commented Leila. "Let me tell you both that Selma had to lose either college or her fiancé for two years. He was ordered to the Philippines to take charge of a naval station on one of the islands. They were to have been married anyway as soon as she was graduated from Hamilton. As it was she chose to go with him. So Selma gained a husband and lost her seniorship and we lost Selma. I shall miss her, for a finer girl never lived."

"Nella will miss her most of all," Vera said quickly. "We must try to make it up to Nella by taking her around with us a lot."

They had by this time reached the Hall. Girl-like they lingered on the steps, enjoying the light night breeze that had sprung up in the last hour. Marjorie's old friend, the chimes, had rung out the stroke of eleven before they reached the Hall. College having not yet opened officially, they claimed the privilege of keeping a little later hours.

As they loitered outside, conversing in low tones, the front door opened and a girl stepped out on the veranda. She uttered a faint sound of surprise at sight of the group of girls. She made a half movement as though to retreat into the house. Then, her face turned away from them, she hurried across the veranda and down the steps.

Though the veranda light was not switched on, the girls had seen her face plainly. To four of them she was known.

"Who was *she* and what ailed her?" was Muriel's light question. "She acted as though she were afraid we might eat her up."

"That was Miss Sayres, President Matthews' private secretary," answered Leila in a peculiar tone. "As to what ailed her, she did not expect to see us and she was not pleased. We have an old Irish proverb: 'When a man runs from you be sure his feet are at odds with his conscience.'"

CHAPTER IV.

A CONGENIAL PAIR

"WELL; here we are at the same old stand again." Leslie Cairns yawned, stretched upward her kimono-clad arms and clasped them behind her head. Lounging opposite her, in a deep, Sleepy-Hollow chair, Natalie Weyman, also in a negligee, scanned her friend's face with some anxiety.

"Les, do you or do you not intend to try to make a new stand this year for our rights? I think the way we were treated last year after that basket-ball affair was simply outrageous. I don't mean by Miss Dean and her crowd, I mean by girls we had lunched and done plenty of favors for."

"If you are talking about the freshies they never were to be depended upon from the first. Bess Walbert stood by us, of course. So did a lot of Alston Terrace kids. She did good work for us there."

"Every reason why she should have," Natalie tartly pointed out. She was still jealous of Leslie's friendship with Elizabeth Walbert. "You did enough for *her*. She certainly will not win the soph presidency, no matter how much you may root for her. She was awfully unpopular with her class before college closed. I know that to be a fact."

"Why is it that you have to go up in the air like a sky rocket every time I mention Bess Walbert's name?" Leslie scowled her impatience. "You wouldn't give that poor kid credit for anything clever she had done, no matter how wonderful it was."

"Humph! I have yet to learn of anything wonderful she ever did or ever will do," sneered Natalie. "I am not going to quarrel with you, Leslie, about her." Natalie modified her tone. "She isn't worth it. You think I am awfully jealous of her. I am not. I don't like her because she is so untruthful."

"Why don't you say she is a liar and be done with it?" 'So untruthful!' Leslie mimicked. "That sounds like Bean and her crowd." Displeased with Natalie for decrying Elizabeth Walbert, Leslie took revenge by mimicking her chum. She knew nothing cut Natalie more than to be mimicked.

"All right. I will say it. Bess Walbert *is* a liar and you will find it out, too, before you are done with her. Besides, she is treacherous. If you were to turn her down for any reason, she wouldn't care what she said about you on the campus. I have watched her a good deal, Les. She's like this.

She will take a little bit of truth for a foundation and then build up something from it that's entirely a lie. If she would stick to facts; but she doesn't."

"She has always been square enough with me," Leslie insisted.

"Because you have made a fuss over her," was the instant explanation. "She knows you are at the head of the Sans and she has taken precious good care to keep in with you. She cares for no one but herself."

"Oh, nonsense! That's what you always said about Lola Elster. I've never had any rows with Lola. We're as good friends today as ever."

"Still Lola dropped you the minute she grew chummy with Alida Burton," Natalie reminded. "Lola was just ungrateful, though. She has more honor in a minute than Bess will ever have. She isn't a talker or a mischief-maker. She never thinks of much but having a good time. She hardly ever says anything gossipy about anyone."

"I thought you didn't like Lola?" Leslie smiled in her slow fashion.

"I don't," came frankly. "Of the two evils, I prefer her to Bess. My advice to you is not to be too pleasant with Bess until you see what her position here at Hamilton is going to be. I tell you she isn't well liked. You can keep her at arm's length, if you begin that way, without making her sore. If

you baby her and then drop her, look out!" Natalie shook a prophetic finger at Leslie.

"We can't afford to take any chances this year,
Les. With all the things we have done that would
put us in line for being expelled, we have managed
by sheer good luck to slide from under. If we
hadn't worked like sixty last spring term to make
up for the time we lost fooling with basket-ball we
wouldn't be seniors now. I don't want any condi-
tions to work off this year."

"Neither do I. Don't intend to have 'em. I
begin to believe you may be right about keeping
Bess in her place." Natalie's evident earnestness
had made some impression on her companion.

"I *know* I am," Natalie emphasized with loft dignity. "Are you sure she doesn't know anything
about that hazing business? She made a remark
to Harriet Stephens last spring that sounded as
though she knew all about it."

"Well, she does not, unless someone of the Sans
besides you or I has told her of it." Leslie sat up
straight in her chair, looking rather worried. "I
must pump her and find out what she knows. If
she does know of it, then we have a traitor in the
camp. Mark me, I'll throw any girl out of the club
who has babbled that affair. Didn't we doubly
swear, afterward, never to tell it to a soul while we
were at Hamilton?"

"Hard to say who told Bess," shrugged Natalie. "Certainly it was not I."

"No; you're excepted. I said that." Leslie's assurance was bored. She was tired of hearing Natalie extol her own loyalty. It was an everyday citation. "That hazing stunt of ours doesn't worry me half so much as that trick we put over on Trotty Remson. I am always afraid that Laura will flivver someday and the whole thing will come to light. If it happens after I leave Hamilton, I don't care. All I care about is getting through. If I keep on the soft side of my father he is going to let me help run his business. That's my dream. But I have to be graduated with honors, if there are any I can pull down. At least I must stick it out here for my diploma."

"What would your father do if you flunked this year in any way?"

"He would disown me. I mean that. I have money of my own; lots of it. That part of it wouldn't feaze me. But my father is the only person on earth I really have any respect for. I'd never get over it; *never.*"

Leslie's loose features showed a tightened intensity utterly foreign to them. Her hands took hold on the chair arms with a grip which revealed something of the nervous emotion the fell contingency inspired in her.

The two girls had arrived on the seven o'clock train from the north that evening. They had stopped at the Lotus for dinner and had reached the hall shortly before the beginning of the sere-nade. Leslie had been Natalie's guest at the Wey-mans' camp in the Adirondacks. Thus the two had come on to college together instead of accepting Dulcie Vale's invitation to journey from New York City to Hamilton in the Vales' private car, as they had done the three previous years. Since the haz-ing party on St. Valentine's night, Leslie and Dulcie had not been on specially good terms. Les-lie was still peeved with Dulcie for not having locked the back door of the untenanted house as she had been ordered to do. Had she obeyed orders the Sans would not have been put to panic-stricken flight by unknown invaders. While those who had come to Marjorie's rescue might have hung about the outside of the house, they could not have found entrance easy with both back and front doors prop-erly locked.

"I don't know what is the matter with me to-night." Leslie rose and commenced a restless walk up and down the room, hands clasped behind her back. "That music upset me, I guess. I wonder who the singers were. Serenading Bean and her gang. Humph! Nobody ever serenaded us that I can recall. I suppose Beanie arrived in all her glory this afternoon, hence those yowlers under her window tonight."

"They really sang beautifully. Whoever played the violin was a fine musician. I never heard a better rendition of 'How Fair Art Thou.'" Fond of music, Natalie was forced to admit the high quality of the performance, even though the serenade had been in honor of the girl of whom she had always been so jealous.

"I don't care much for music unless it is ragtime or musical comedy stuff. Sentimental songs get on my nerves. I hate that priggish old 'Hymn to Hamilton.' I hope Laura got out of here without being seen." Leslie went back to the subject still uppermost in her mind. "It was risking something to send for her to come over here, but I was anxious to see her and find out if anything had happened this summer detrimental to us. I didn't feel like meeting her along the road tonight."

"Oh, I don't believe anyone saw her," reassured Natalie. "It was after eleven when she left here. The house was quiet as could be. I noticed it when I went out in the hall before she left to see if the coast was clear. Not more than half the girls who belong here are back yet. Bean and her crowd had gone to bed, I presume. You wouldn't catch such angels as they even making a dent in the ten-thirty rule."

"That's so." Leslie made one more trip up and down the room, then resumed the chair in which she had been sitting. "Well, I'll take it for granted that Sayres made a clean get-away. One thing about her, she will stand by us as long as she is paid for it. Besides, she would get into more trouble than we if the truth were known. That's where we have the advantage of her. She has to protect herself as well as us. What I have always been afraid of is this: If Remson and old Doctor Know-it-all ever came to an understanding he would go to quizzing Sayres. If she lost her nerve, for he is a terror when he's angry, she might flivver."

"Don't cross bridges until you come to them," counseled Natalie. She was beginning to see the value of assuming the role of comforter to Leslie. One thing Natalie had determined. She would strain a point to be first with Leslie during their senior year. She had importuned Leslie to visit her for the purpose of regaining her old footing. She and Leslie had spent a fairly congenial month together in the Adirondacks. Now Natalie intended to hold the ground she had gained against all comers.

"I'm not going to. I shall forget last year, so far as I can. I certainly spent enough money and didn't gain a thing. Our best plan is to go on as we did last spring. If I see a good opportunity to bother Bean and her devoted beanstalks, I shall not let it pass me by. I am not going to take any more risks, though. If I manage to live down those I've taken, I'll do well."

"I know I wouldn't *raise a hand* to help a freshie this year," Natalie declared with a positive pucker of her small mouth. "Think of the way we rushed the greedy ingrates! Then they wouldn't stand up for us during that basket-ball trouble."

"Put all that down to profit and loss." Leslie had emerged from the brief spasm of dread which invariably visited her after seeing Laura Sayres. "We had the wrong kind of girls to deal with. There were more digs and prigs in that class than eligibles. That's why we lost. I am all done with that sort of thing. If I can't be as popular as Bean," Leslie's intonation was bitterly sarcastic, "I can be a good deal more exclusive. As it is, I expect to have all I can do to keep the Sans in line. Dulcie Vale has an idea that she ought to run the club. Give her a chance and she'd run it into the ground. She has as much sense as a peacock. She can fan her feathers and squawk."

Natalie laughed outright at this. It was so exactly descriptive of Dulcie.

Leslie looked well pleased with herself. She thoroughly enjoyed saying smart things which made people laugh. It was a sore cross to her that after three years of the hardest striving she had not attained the kind of popularity at Hamilton which she craved. Yet she could not see wherein she was to blame.

Gifted with a keen sense of humor, she had tricks of expression so original in themselves that she might have easily gained a reputation as the funniest girl in college. Had good humor radiated her peculiarly rugged features she would have been that rarity, an ugly beauty. Due to her proficiency at golf and tennis, she was of most symmetrical figure. She was particularly fastidious as to dress, and made a smart appearance. Having so much that was in her favor, she was hopelessly hampered by, self.

CHAPTER V

A LUCKY MISHAP

THE serenading expedition of the next night was the beginning of a succession of similar gaieties for the Lookouts. As Hamilton continued to gather in her own for the college year, the Sanford quintette found themselves in flattering demand.

"If I don't stay at home once in a while I shall never be able to find a thing that belongs to me," Muriel Harding cried out in despair as Jerry reminded her at luncheon that they were invited to Silverton Hall that evening to celebrate Elaine Hunter's birthday. "You girls may laugh, but honestly I haven't finished unpacking my trunk. Every time I plan to wind up that delightful job, along comes some friendly, but misguided person and invites me out."

"Stay at home then," advised Jerry. "If that last remark of yours was meant for me, I am *not* misguided and I shall *not* be friendly if you hurl such adjectives at me."

"Neither was meant for you. You are only the bearer of the invitation. Why stir up a breeze over nothing?"

"If you don't go to Elaine's birthday party she will think you stayed away because you were too stingy to buy her a present. We are all going to drive to Hamilton this afternoon after classes to buy gifts for her. Don't you wish you were going, too?" Ronny regarded Muriel with tantalizing eyes.

"Oh, I'm going along," Muriel glibly assured. "You can't lose me. What I like to do and what I ought to do are two very different things. After this week I shall settle down to the student life in earnest. My subjects are terrific this term. I am sorry I started calculus. I had enough to do without that."

"This will have to be my last party for a week or two," Marjorie declared. "I haven't done any real studying this week, and I owe all my correspondents letters. I feel guilty for not having done more toward helping this years' freshies. I've only been down to the station twice."

"They're in good hands. Phil and Barbara have done glorious work. They have had at least twenty sophs helping them. It's a cinch this year. Very different from last." Jerry gave a short laugh. "Phil says," Jerry discreetly lowered her voice, "that not a Sans has come near the station since she has been on committee duty there to welcome the freshies. I told her it didn't surprise me."

"I didn't know Miss Cairns and Miss Weyman had come back until I happened to pass them in the upstairs hall," Muriel said.

"They were here for a couple of days before Leila knew it, and she generally knows who is back and who isn't. Miss Remson told Leila she didn't know it herself until the next day after they arrived. The two of them came back together on the night we were serenaded. They simply walked into the house and went to their rooms. She didn't see them until noon the next day." It was Veronica who delivered this information.

"Did Miss Remson say anything to them on account of it?" questioned Muriel.

"No; she wasn't pleased, but she said she thought it best to ignore it. It was just one more discourtesy on their part."

"That accounts for our meeting Miss Sayres on the veranda." Lucy's greenish eyes had grown speculative. "She had been calling on those two. We spoke of it after she passed, you will remember. Leila said 'No,' they had not come back yet. We wondered on whom she had been calling at the Hall. While we can't prove that it was Miss Cairns and Miss Weyman she had come to see, that would be the natural conclusion," Lucy summed up, with the gravity of a lawyer.

"I object, your honor. The evidence is too fragmentary to be considered," put in Muriel in mannish tones. She bowed directly to Marjorie.

"Court's adjourned. I have nothing to say." Marjorie laughed and pushed back her chair from the table. I'm not making light of what you said, Lucy." She turned to the latter. "I was only funning with Muriel. I think as you do. Still none of us can prove it."

"I wish the whole thing would be cleared up before those girls are graduated and gone from Hamilton," Katherine Langly said almost vindictively. "I wouldn't care if it made a lot of trouble for them all. Miss Remson has stood so much from them and she still feels so hurt at Doctor Matthews' unjust treatment of her. I can't believe he wrote that letter. She believes it."

"I don't see how she can in face of all the contemptible things the Sans have done," asserted Jerry.

"She believes it because she says he signed the letter, so he must have written it. I told her the signature might be a forgery. She said 'No, it could hardly be that.' I saw she was set on that point, so I didn't argue it further."

"Excuse me for abruptly changing the subject, but where are we to meet after classes this P. M.?" inquired Muriel.

The chums had left the table and proceeded as far as the hall, where their ways separated.

"Go straight over to the garage. Our two Old Reliables will be there with their buzz wagons. Be on time, too," called Jerry, as with an "All right, much obliged, Jeremiah," Muriel started up the stairs. Half way up she turned and asked, "What time?"

"Quarter past four. If you aren't there on the dot we shall go without you. None of us know what we are going to buy, so we want all the time we can have to look around. Remember, we have to hustle back to the Hall, have dinner and dress."

"I'll remember." With a wag of her head Muriel

resumed her ascent of the stairs and quickly disappeared.

The others stopped briefly in the hall to talk. Marjorie was next to leave the group. She remembered she had intended to change her white linen frock, which did not look quite fresh enough for a trip to town. Her last recitation of the afternoon being chemistry, she knew she would have no time to return to the Hall before meeting her chums at the garage.

Alas for the pretty gown of delft blue pongee which she had donned with girlish satisfaction at luncheon time. An accident at the chemical desk sent a veritable deluge of discoloring liquid showering over her. Despite her apron, her frock was plentifully spotted by it.

Ordinarily she would have made light of the misfortune. As it was she felt ready to cry with vexation. She would have to change gowns again in order to be presentable for the trip to Hamilton. The girls had set four-fifteen as the starting time. She could not possibly make it before four-thirty.

Her first resolve was to hurry over to the garage immediately after the chemistry period and tell the the girls not to wait for her.

In spite of Jerry's assertion to Muriel that they would not wait a moment after four-fifteen, Marjorie knew that they would strain a point and linger a little longer if she did not put in an appearance at the time appointed. Recalling the fact that Lucy was in the Biological Laboratory, situated across the hall from the Chemical Laboratory, Marjorie decided to try to catch Lucy before she left the building and send word to the others to go on without her. She could then hurry straight to the Hall, slip into another gown and hail a taxicab going to the town of Hamilton. There were usually two or three to be found in the immediate vicinity of the campus.

"Oh, there you are!" Marjorie hailed softly, when, at precisely four o'clock Lucy emerged from the laboratory across the hall. I thought you would be out on the minute on account of going to town. I left chemistry five minutes earlier for fear of missing you. Just see what happened to me." She displayed the results of the accident. "I am a sight. Tell the girls not to wait. I must go on to the Hall and make myself presentable. I'll take a taxi and meet them at the Curio Shop. If they're ready to go on before I reach there, tell them to leave word with the proprietor where they are going next."

"All right. What a shame about your dress. Do you think those stains will come out?" Lucy scanned the unsightly spots and streaks with a dubious eye.

"I know they won't." Marjorie voiced rueful

positiveness. "This is the first time I ever wore this frock. I gave it a nice baptism, didn't I? Well, it can't be helped now. I mustn't stop." The two had come to the outer entrance to Science Hall. "See you at the Curio Shop." With a parting wave of the hand Marjorie ran lightly down the steps and trotted across the campus.

Always quick of action, it did not take her long, once she had gained her room, to discard the unlucky blue pongee gown for one of pink linen.

"Just half-past four. I didn't do so badly," she congratulated, consulting her wrist watch as she hastened down the driveway toward the west gate. "Now for a taxi."

No taxicab was in sight, however. Three of these useful vehicles had recently reaped a harvest of students bound for town and started off with them. Five minutes passed and Marjorie grew more impatient. To undertake to walk to Hamilton would add greatly to the delay in joining the gift seekers. True she might meet a taxicab on the way. Whether the driver would turn back for a single fare she was not sure. She determined to walk on rather than stand still. If she were lucky enough to meet a taxicab on the highway she would offer its driver double fare to turn around and take her into town.

The brisk pace at which she walked soon brought

her to the western end of the campus wall. Presently she had reached the beginning of Hamilton Estates. And still no sign of a taxicab!

"It looks as though I'd have to walk after all," she remarked, half aloud. "How provoking!" She would reach the Curio Shop about the time the others were starting for the campus was her vexed calculation. Besides, there was Lucy, who would patiently wait for her when she might be going on with the others. They had planned to visit two or three shops.

In the midst of her annoyance, the sound of a motor behind caused her to turn. To her surprise she recognized the driver and machine as being of the regular jitney service between the campus and the town. His only fare was a young man, evidently a salesman who had had business at the college. He was occupying the front seat beside the driver.

The latter stopped at Marjorie's sign and opened the door of the tonneau for her. Very thankfully she stepped in. Engaged in conversation with the salesman, the man at the wheel drove along at a leisurely rate of speed. Marjorie could only wish that he would hurry a little faster.

Coming opposite to Hamilton Arms, Marjorie forgot her impatience as her eyes eagerly took in the estate she so greatly admired. The chrysanthemums had begun to throw out luxuriant bloom in border and bed, while the bronze and scarlet of fallen leaves lay lightly on the short-cropped grass.

Almost opposite the point where Hamilton Arms adjoined the next estate, Marjorie spied a small, familiar figure trotting along at the left of the highway. It was Miss Susanna Hamilton. In one hand she carried a good-sized splint basket from which nodded a colorful wealth of chrysanthemums in little individual flower pots. She was bare-headed, though over her black silk dress she wore the knitted scarlet shawl which gave her the odd likeness to a lively old robin.

Marjorie leaned forward a trifle as the machine came opposite Miss Susanna. She viewed the last of the Hamiltons with kindly, non-curious eyes. The taxicab had almost slid past the sturdy pedestrian when something happened. The handle of the splint basket treacherously gave way, landing the basket on the ground with force. It tipped side-ways. Two or three of the flower pots rolled out of it.

Forgetting everything but the mishap to Brooke Hamilton's eccentric descendant, Marjorie called out on impulse: "Driver; please stop the taxi! I wish to get out here!"

CHAPTER VI

THE LAST OF THE HAMILTONS

THE man promptly brought the machine to a slow stop. He was too well acquainted with the whims of "them girls from the college" to exhibit surprise. Having paid her fare on entering the taxicab, Marjorie now quitted it with alacrity and ran back to the scene of the mishap.

"Please let me help you," she offered in a gracious fashion which came straight from her heart. "I saw the handle of that basket break and I made the driver stop and let me out of the taxi."

Without waiting for Miss Susanna's permission, Marjorie stooped and lay hold on one of the scattered flower pots. Thus far the old lady had made no effort to gather them in. She had stood eyeing the unstable basket with marked disgust.

"And who are you, may I ask?" The brisk manner of question reminded Marjorie of Miss Remson.

"Oh, I am Marjorie Dean from Hamilton College," Marjorie said, straightening up with a smile.

For an instant the two pairs of dark eyes met. In the old lady's appeared a gleam half resentful, half admiring. In the young girl's shone a pleasant light, hard to resist.

"Yes; I supposed you were one of them," nodded Miss Susanna. "Let me tell you, young woman, you are the first I have met in all these years from the college who had any claim on gentle breeding."

Marjorie smiled. "There are a good many fine girls at Hamilton," she defended without intent to be discourteous. "Any one of a number I know would have been glad to help you."

"Then that doll shop has changed a good deal recently," retorted the old lady with rapidity. "Nowadays it is nothing but drive flamboyant cars and spend money for frivolities over there. I hate the place."

Marjorie was silent. She did not like to contradict further by saying pointedly that she loved Hamilton, neither could she bear the thought of not defending her Alma Mater.

"I can't say that I hate Hamilton College, because I don't," she finally returned, before the pause between the two had grown embarassing. "I am sure you must have good reason to dislike Hamilton and its students or you would not say so."

The pink in her cheeks deepened. Marjorie bent

and completed the task of returning the last spilled posy to the basket.

"There!" she exclaimed good-naturedly. "I have them all in the basket again, and not a single one of those little jars are broken. I wish you would let me carry the basket for you, Miss Hamilton. It is really a cumbersome affair without the handle."

"You are quite a nice child, I must say." Miss Susanna continued to regard Marjorie with her bright, bird-like gaze. "Where on earth were you brought up?"

Signally amused, Marjorie laughed outright. She had raised the basket from the ground. As she stood there, her lovely face full of light and laughter, arms full of flowers, Miss Susanna's stubborn old heart softened a trifle toward girlhood.

"I come from Sanford, New York," she answered. "This is my junior year at Hamilton. Four other girls from Sanford entered when I did."

"Sanford," repeated her questioner. "I never heard of the place. If these girls are friends of yours I suppose they escape being barbarians."

"They are the finest girls I ever knew," Marjorie praised with sincerity.

"Well, well; I am pleased to hear it." The old lady spoke with a brusquerie which seemed to indicate her wish to be done with the subject. "You insist on helping me, do you?"

"Yes; if it pleases you to allow me."

"It's to my advantage, so it ought to," was the dry retort. "I am not particular about lugging that basket in my arms. I loaded it too heavily. Brian, the gardener, would have carried it for me, but I didn't care to be bothered with him. I am carrying these down to an old man who used to work about the lawns. His days are numbered and he loves flowers better than anything else. He lives in a little house just outside the estate. It is still quite a walk. If you have anything else to do you had better consider it and not me."

"I was on my way to town. It is too late to go now." Marjorie explained the nature of her errand as they walked on. "The girls will probably come to the conclusion that I found it too late to go to Hamilton after I had changed my gown. One or another of them will buy me something pretty to give to Elaine," she ended.

"It is a good many years since I bought a birthday gift for anyone. I always give my servants money on their birthdays. I have not received a birthday gift for over fifty years and I don't want one. I do not allow my household to make me presents on any occasion." Miss Susanna announced this with a touch of defiance.

"It seems as though my life has been full of presents. My father and mother have given me hundreds, I guess. My father is away from home a good deal. When he comes back from his long business trips he always brings Captain and I whole stacks of treasures."

Marjorie was not sure that this was what she should have said. She found conversing with the last of the Hamiltons a trifle hazardous. She had no desire to contradict, yet she and her new acquaintance had thus far not agreed on a single point.

"Who is 'Captain,'" was the inquiry, made with the curiosity of a child.

Marjorie turned rosy red. The pet appellation had slipped out before she thought.

"I call my mother 'Captain,'" she informed, then went on to explain further of their fond home play. She fully expected Miss Susanna would criticize it as "silly." She was already understanding a little of the lonely old gentlewoman's bitterness of heart. Her earnest desire to know the last of the Hamiltons had arisen purely out of her great sympathy for Miss Susanna.

"You seem to have had a childhood," was the surprising reception her explanation called forth. "I can't endure the children of today. They are grown up in their minds at seven. I must say your

father and mother are exceptional. No wonder you
have good manners. That is, if they are genuine.
I have seen some good imitations. Young girls are
more deceitful than young men. I don't like either.
There is nothing I despise so much as the calloused
selfishness of youth. It is far worse than crabbed
age."

"I know young girls are often selfish of their own
pleasure," Marjorie returned with sudden humility.
"I try not to be. I know I am at times. Many of
my girl friends are not. I wish I could begin to
tell you of the beautiful, unselfish things some of
my chums have done for others."

Miss Susanna vouchsafed no reply to this little
speech. She trotted along beside Marjorie for several rods without saying another word. When she
spoke again it was to say briefly: "Here is where
we turn off the road. Is that basket growing very
heavy?"

"It is quite heavy. I believe I will set it down
for a minute." Marjorie carefully deposited her
burden on the grass at the roadside and straightened up, stretching her aching arms. The basket
had begun to be considerable of a burden on account
of the manner in which it had to be carried.

"I couldn't have lugged that myself," Miss Susanna confessed. "I found it almost too much for
me with the handle on. Ridiculous, the flimsy way

in which things are put together today! Splint baskets of years ago would have stood any amount of strain. If you had not kindly come to my assistance, I intended to pick out as many of those jars as I could carry in my arms and go on with them. The others I would have set up against my own property fence and hoped no one would walk off with them before my return. I dislike anyone to have the flowers I own and have tended unless I give them away myself."

"I have often seen you working among your flowers when I have passed Hamilton Arms. I knew you must love them dearly or you would not spend so much time with them."

"Hm-m!" The interjection might have been an assent to Marjorie's polite observation. It was not, however. Miss Susanna was understanding that this young girl who had shown her such unaffected courtesy had thought of her kindly as a stranger. She experienced a sudden desire to see Marjorie again. Her long and concentrated hatred against Hamilton College and its students forbade her to make any friendly advances. She had already shown more affability according to her ideas than she had intended. She wondered why she had not curtly refused Marjorie's offer.

"I am rested now." Marjorie lifted the basket. The two skirted the northern boundary of Hamil-

ton Arms, taking a narrow private road which lay
between it and the neighboring estate. The road
continued straight to a field where it ended. At the
edge of the field stood a small cottage painted
white. Miss Susanna pointed it out as their destination.

"I will carry this to the door and then leave you."
Marjorie had no desire to intrude upon Miss
Susanna's call at the cottage.

"Very well. I am obliged to you, Marjorie
Dean." Miss Susanna's thanks were expressed in
tones which sounded close to unfriendly. She was
divided between appreciation of Marjorie's courtesy and her dislike for girls.

"You are welcome." They were now within a
few yards of the cottage. Arriving at the low doorstep, Marjorie set the basket carefully upon it.
"Goodbye, Miss Hamilton." She held out her
hand. "I am so glad to have met you."

"What's that? Oh, yes." The old lady took
Marjorie's proffered hand. The evident sincerity
of the words touched a hidden spring within, long
sealed. "Goodbye, child. I am glad to have met
at least one young girl with genuine manners."

Marjorie smiled as she turned away. She had
never before met an old person who so heartily
detested youth. She knew her timely assistance
had been appreciated. On that very account Miss

Susanna had tried to smother, temporarily, her standing grudge against the younger generation.

Well, it had happened. She had achieved her heart's desire. She had actually met and talked with the last of the Hamiltons.

CHAPTER VII

TWO KINDS OF GIRLS

"You are a dandy," was Jerry's greeting as Marjorie walked into their room at ten minutes past six. "Where were you? Lucy said you ruined your blue pongee with some horrid old chemical. It didn't take you two hours to change it, did it? I see we have on our pink linen."

"You know perfectly well it did not take me two hours to change it. A plain insinuation that I'm a slowpoke. Take it back." In high good humor, Marjorie made a playful rush at her room-mate.

"Hold on. I am not made of wood, as Hal says when I occasionally hammer him in fun." Jerry put up her hands in comic self-defense. "You certainly are in a fine humor after keeping your poor pals waiting for you for an hour and a half and then not even condescending to appear."

"I've had an adventure, Jeremiah. That's why I didn't meet you girls in Hamilton. I started for there in a taxicab. Then I met a lady in distress, and, emulating the example of a gallant knight, I hopped out of the taxi to help her."

"Wonderful! I suppose you met Phil Moore or some other Silvertonite with her arms full of bundles. About the time she saw you she dropped 'em. 'With a sympathetic yell, Helpful Marjorie leaped from the taxicab to aid her overburdened but foolish friend.' Quotation from the last best seller." Jerry regarded Marjorie with a teasing smile.

"Your suppositions are about a mile off the track. I haven't seen a Silvertonite this afternoon. The lady in distress I met was——" Marjorie paused by way of making her revelation more effective, "Miss Susanna Hamilton."

"*What?* You don't say so." Jerry exhibited the utmost astonishment. "Good thing you didn't ask me to guess. She is the last person I would have thought of. Now how did it happen? I am glad of it for your sake. You've been so anxious to know her."

Rapidly Marjorie recounted the afternoon's adventure. As she talked she busied herself with the redressing of her hair. After dinner she would have no more than time to put on the white lingerie frock she intended to wear to Elaine's birthday party.

Jerry listened without comment. While she had never taken the amount of interest in the owner of Hamilton Arms which Marjorie had evinced since entering Hamilton College, she had a certain curiosity regarding Miss Susanna.

"I knew you girls would wait and wonder what had delayed me. I am awfully sorry. You know that, Jeremiah," Marjorie apologized. "But I couldn't have gone on in the taxi after I saw what had happened to Miss Susanna. She couldn't have carried the basket as I did clear over to that cottage. She said she would have picked up as many plant jars as she could carry in her arms and gone on with them."

"One of the never-say-die sort, isn't she? Very likely in the years she has lived near the college she has met with some rude girls. On the order of the Sans, you know. If, in the past twenty years, Hamilton was half as badly overrun with snobs as when we entered, one can imagine why she doesn't adore students."

"It doesn't hurt my feelings to hear her say she disliked girls. I only felt sorry for her. It must be dreadful to be old and lonely. She is lonely, even if she doesn't know it. She has deliberately shut the door between herself and happiness. I am so glad we're young, Jeremiah." Marjorie sighed her gratitude for the gift of youth. "I hope always to be young at heart."

"I sha'n't wear a cap and spectacles and walk with a cane until I have to, believe me," was Jerry's emphatic rejoinder. "Are you ready to go down to dinner? My hair is done, too. I shall dress after I've been fed. Oh, I forgot to tell you. I bought you a present to give Elaine. We bought every last thing we are going to give her at the Curio Shop."

"You are a dear. I knew some of the girls would help me out. I supposed it would be you, though. Do let me see my present."

"There it is on my chiffonier. You'd better examine it after dinner. It is a hand-painted chocolate pot; a beauty, too. Looks like a bit of spring time."

"I'll look at it the minute I come back. I'm oceans obliged to you." Marjorie cast a longing glance at the tall package on the chiffonier, as the two girls left the room.

At dinner that night Marjorie's adventure of the afternoon excited the interest of her chums. She was obliged to repeat, as nearly as she could what she said to Miss Susanna and what Miss Susanna had said to her.

"Did she mention the May basket?" quizzed Muriel with a giggle.

"Now why should she?" counter-questioned Marjorie.

"Well; she was talking about not receiving a birthday present for over fifty years. She might have said, 'But some kind-hearted person hung a beautiful violet basket on my door on May day evening!'"

"Only she didn't. That flight of fancy was wasted," Jerry informed Muriel.

"Wasted on you. You haven't proper sentiment," flung back Muriel.

"I'll never acquire it in your company," Jerry assured. The subdued laughter the tilt evoked reached the table occupied by Leslie Cairns, Natalie Weyman, Dulcie Vale and three others of the Sans.

"Those girls seem to find enough to laugh at," commented Dulcie Vale half enviously.

"Simpletons!" muttered Leslie Cairns. She was out of sorts with the world in general that evening. "They sit there and 'ha-ha-ha' at their meals until I can hardly stand it sometimes. I hate eating dinner here. I'd dine at the Colonial every evening, but it takes too much time. I really must study hard this year to get through. I certainly will be happy to see the last of this treadmill. I'm going to take a year after I'm graduated just to sail around and have a good time. After that I shall help my father in business."

"There's one thing you ought to know, Leslie, and that is you had better be careful what you do this year. I have heard two or three rumors that sound as though those girls over there had told about what happened the night of the masquerade. I wouldn't take part in another affair of that kind for millions of dollars."

Dulcie Vale assumed an air of virtuous resolve as she delivered herself of this warning to Leslie.

"Don't worry. There won't be any occasion. I don't believe those muffs ever told a thing outside of their own crowd. They're a close corporation. I wish I could say the same of us." Leslie laughed this arrow with cool deliberation.

"What do you mean?" Harriet Stephens said sharply. "Who of us would be silly enough to tell our private affairs?"

"I hope you wouldn't." Leslie's eyes narrowed threateningly. "I have heard one or two things myself which may or may not be true. I am not ready to say anything further just now. My advice to all of you is to keep your affairs to yourselves. If you are foolish enough to babble your own about the campus, on your head be it. Be sure you will hear from me if you tell tales. Besides, you are apt to lose your diplomas by it. A word to the wise, you know. I have a recitation in psychology in the morning. I must put in a quiet evening. Kindly let me alone, all of you." She rose and sauntered from the room, leaving her satellites to discuss her open insinuation and wonder what she had heard to put her in such an "outrageous" humor.

CHAPTER VIII

A FROLIC AT SILVERTON HALL

THE "simpletons" finished their dinner amid much merriment, quite unconscious of their lack of sense, and hustled up to their rooms to dress for the party. Leila, Vera, Helen, Hortense Barlow, Eva Ingram, Nella Sherman and Mary Cornell had also been invited. Shortly after seven the elect started for Silverton Hall, primed for a jubilant evening. Besides their gifts, each girl carried a small nosegay of mixed flowers. The flowers had been purchased in bulk by Helen, Eva and Mary. The trio had made them up into dainty, round bouquets. These were to be showered upon Elaine, immediately she appeared among them. Helen had also composed a Nonsense Ode which she said had cost her more mental effort than forty themes.

Every girl at Silverton Hall was invited to the party. It was not in gentle Elaine to slight anyone. With twenty girls from other campus houses, the long living room at the Hall was filled. Across one of its lower corners had been hung a heavy green curtain. What it concealed only those who had arranged the surprise knew. Elaine had been seized by Portia Graham and Blanche Scott and made to swear on her sacred honor that she would absolutely shun the living room until granted permission to enter it.

"I hope you have all put cards with your presents," were Portia's first words after greeting them at the door. "You can't give them to Elaine yourselves. We've arranged a general presentation. So don't be snippy because I rob you of your offerings."

"Glad of it." Jerry promptly tendered her gift to Portia. "I always feel silly giving a present."

The others from Wayland Hall very willingly surrendered their good-will offerings. Their bouquets they kept. Entering the reception hall, Elaine stepped forward to welcome them and received a sudden flower pelting, to the accompaniment of a lively chorus of congratulations.

"How lovely! Umm! The dear things!" she exclaimed, as the rain of blossoms came fast and furious. Her sweet, fair face aglow with the love of flowers, she gathered them up in the overskirt of her white chiffon frock and sat down on the lower step of the stairs to enjoy their fragrance. "I am not allowed in the living room, girls. Everyone can go in there but poor me. I thank you for these perfectly darling bouquets. I'll have a different one to wear every day this week. If you want to fix your hair or do any further beautifying go up to Robin's room. If not, go into the living room."

Lingering for a little further chat with Elaine, whom they all adored, they entered the living room to be met by a vociferous welcome from the assembled Silvertonites. When the last guest had arrived and been ushered into the reception room, from somewhere in the house a bell suddenly tinkled. In order to give more space the chairs had been removed and the guests lined the sides of the apartment and filled one end of it halfway to the wide doorway opening into the main hall.

At sound of the bell a hush fell upon the merrymakers. Again it tinkled and down the stairs came a procession that might have stepped from a tapestry depicting the life of the greenwood men. Four merry men, their green cambric costumes carefully modeled after the attire of Robin Hood and his followers, had come to the party. The first, instead of being Robin Hood, was Robin Page.

She bowed low to Elaine, who was still languishing in exile in the hall, and offered her arm.

"Delighted; I am so tired of hanging about that old hall!" Elaine seized Robin's arm with alacrity and the two passed into the adjoining room. The other three faithful servitors followed their leader. The last one carried a violin and drew from it an old-time greenwood melody as Elaine and Robin joined forces and paraded into the living room.

Straight toward the green curtain Robin piloted Elaine to the fiddler's plaintive tune. Stationed before the curtain, Blanche Scott drew it aside.

A surprised and admiring chorus of exclamations arose. There stood a real greenwood tree. Portia and Blanche could have amply testified to this fact as the two of them, armed with a hatchet, had laboriously chopped down a small maple and brought it to the house from the woods on the afternoon previous. Its branches were as well loaded with packages of various sizes as those of a Christmas tree. Under the tree was a grassy mound built up of hard cushions, the whole covered with real sod dug up by the patient wood cutters.

On this Elaine was invited to sit. She formed a pretty picture in her fluffy white gown in conjunction with the greenery. The four merry men gathered round her and bowed low, then sang her an ancient ballad to the accompaniment of the violin. Followed a short speech by the tallest of the four congratulating her, in stately language on the anniversary of her birth. Three of the four then busied themselves with stripping the tree of its spoils and laying them at her feet. During this procedure the fiddler evoked further sweet thin melodies from his violin.

Last, Elaine's gallant escort, who had left her briefly, returned to the scene with a large green and white straw basket, piled high with gifts. These duly presented, the quaint bit of forest play was over and the enjoying spectators crowded about the lucky recipient of friendly riches.

"I don't know what I shall ever do with them all," she declared in an amazed, quavering voice. "I'm not half over the shock of so much wealth yet. I simply can't open them now. I'll weep tears of gratitude over every separate one of them."

"You aren't expected to look at them now," was Robin's reassurance. "Your merry men are going to carry Elaine's nice new playthings up to her room. So there! Tomorrow's Saturday. You can spend the afternoon exploring. We are going to have a stunt party now. Anyone who is called upon to do a stunt has to conform or be ostracized."

"If we are going to do stunts there is no use in bringing back the chairs. After Elaine's presents

have all been carted upstairs everybody can stand in
that half of the room. We can roll the rug up
from the other end exactly half way. That will
give room and a smooth floor for dancing stunts.
We shall surely have some," planned Blanche. "I
had better inform the company of what's going to
happen next. It will give them a chance to think
up a stunt."

While the faithful greenwood men busied themselves in Elaine's behalf, Blanche proceeded to
make a humorous address to the guests. Her an-
nouncement sent them into a flutter. At least half
of the crowd protested to her and to one another
that they did not know any stunts to perform.

When the deck was finally clear for action and
the show began, it was amazing the number of
funny little stunts that came to light. The first girl
called upon was Hortense Barlow. She marched
solemnly to the center of the improvised stage and
announced " 'Home Sweet Home,' by our domestic
animals." A rooster lustily crowed the first few
bars of the old song, then two hens took it up.
They relinquished it in favor of a bleating lamb.
It was succeeded by a pair of grunting pigs. The
opening bars of the chorus were mournfully
"mooed" by a lonely cow, and the rest of it was
ably sung by a donkey, a dog and a guinea hen.

She then repeated the chorus as a concerted effort on the part of the barnyard denizens.

The manner in which she managed to imitate each creature, still keeping fairly in tune, was clever in the extreme. Her final concert chorus convulsed her audience and she was obliged to repeat it.

Hers was the only encore allowed. Portia announced that, owing to the lack of time, encores would have to be dispensed with. The guests had received permission to be out of their house until half-past eleven and no later.

Leila was the next on the list and responded with an old-time Irish jig. Vera Ingram and Mary Cornell gave a brief singing and dancing sketch. Jerry responded with the one stunt she could do to perfection. She had half closed her eyes, opened her mouth to its widest extent, and wailed a popular song just enough off the key to be funny. Heartily detesting this class of melody, she never failed to make her chums laugh with her mocking imitation.

Portia being in charge of the stunt programme, she called upon Blanche who gave the "Prologue from Pagliacci" in a baritone voice and with expression which would have done credit to an opera singer. Lucy Warner surprised her chums by a fine recital of "The Chambered Nautilus," giving the quiet dramatic emphasis needed to bring out Holmes' poem. Marie Peyton danced a fisher's

hornpipe. Vera Mason borrowed one of Robin's
kimonos and a fan and performed a Japanese fan
dance. Several of the Silvertonites sang, danced,
recited, or told a humorous story.

"As we shall have time for only one more stunt,
I will call on Ronny Lynne," Portia announced,
smiling invitingly at Ronny. "Wait a minute until
I call the orchestra together. We will play for
you," she added.

"Play for me for what?" Ronny innocently inquired. Nevertheless she laughed. Though she
had yet to dance for the first time at Hamilton, she
knew that her ability as a dancer was an open secret.

"For your dance, of course. What kind of dance
are you going to do? Mustn't refuse. Everyone
else has been so obliging." Portia beamed triumph
of having thus neatly caught Ronny.

"I suppose I must fall in line. I don't know what
to dance. Most of my dances require special costumes." Ronny glanced dubiously at the white and
gold evening frock she was wearing. "I know one
I can do," she said, after a moment's thought.

Raising her voice so as to be heard by all, she
continued in her clear tones: "Girls, I am going to
do a Russian interpretative dance for you. The
idea is this: A dancer at the court of a king, who
is honored because of her art, loses her sweetheart.
She becomes so despondent that no amount of

praise can lift her from her gloom. She tries to decide whether she had best kill her rival or herself. Finally she decides to kill her rival. I shall endeavor to make this plain in a dance containing two intervals and three episodes. The first depicts the dancer in her glory. The second, in her dejection. The third, her decision to kill."

A brief consultation with the orchestra as to what they could play, suitable to the interpretation, and Ronny was ready. Phyllis, the reliable, who had been proficient on the violin from childhood, and possessed a wide musical repertoire, both vocal and instrumental, played over a few measures of a *valse lente*. Her musicians were familiar enough with it to follow her lead. Moskowski's "Serenade" was chosen for the second episode, and Scharwenki's "Polish Dance" for the third.

Every pair of eyes was centered on Ronny's slight, graceful figure as she stood at ease for an instant waiting for the music to begin. Many of the girls present had never seen an interpretative dance. With the first slow, seductive strains of the waltz, Ronny became the court dancer. In perfect time to the music she made the low sweeping salutes to an imaginary court, then executed a swaying, beautiful dance of intricate steps in which her whole body seemed to take part in the expression of her art. The grace of that symphonic,

white and gold figure was such the watchers held
their breath. At the end of the episode there was a
dead silence. Applause, when it came, was deaf-
ening.

Ronny claimed the tiny interval for rest, merely
raising her hands in a despairing gesture at the
hub-bub her dance had created. By the time she
was ready to continue it had subsided. All were
now anxious to see her interpretation of the jilted
woman.

The second, though much harder to execute,
Ronny liked far better than the first. Particularly
fond of the Russian idea of the dance, she threw
her whole heart into the story she was endeavoring
to convey by motion. When she had finished she
was tired enough to gladly claim a rest while Portia
went upstairs for a paper knife which would serve
as a dagger for the third episode.

The wild strains of the "Polish Dance" were
well suited to the character of the episode. The
flitting, white and gold figure of indolent grace had
now become one of tense purpose. Every line of
her figure had now become charged with the desire
for revenge. Every step of the dance and movement of the arms were in accordance with the mood
she was portraying. She enacted the dancer's plan
to steal upon her rival unawares and deliver the
fatal knife thrust.

Had Ronny not explained the dance beforehand, so vivid was her interpretation, her audience could have gained the meaning of it without difficulty. A united sighing breath of appreciation went up as she concluded the Terpsichorean tragedy by a triumphant flinging of her arms above her head, one hand tightly grasping the murder knife.

Carried out of life ordinary by the glimpse of another world of emotion, it took the admiring girls a minute or so to realize that Ronny was herself and a fellow student. She had cast over them the perfect illusion of the tragic dancer; the sure measure of her art. When they came out of it they crowded about her asking all sorts of eager questions.

"Ronny has brought down the house, as usual. Look at those girls fairly idolizing her." Jerry's round face was wreathed with smiles over Ronny's triumph. "I shall go in for interpretative dancing myself, hereafter. It's about time I did something to make myself popular around here."

"What are you going to interpret?" Muriel demanded to know.

"I haven't yet decided," Jerry vaguely replied. "Anyway, I wouldn't tell you if I had. I should expect to practice my dance awhile before I sprang it on anyone. It might give my victim a horrible scare."

"You wouldn't scare me," was the valorous assurance. "You had better try it on me first when you are ready to burst upon the world as a dancer. I will give you valuable ciriticism."

"Laugh at me, you mean. Come on. Let's interview the orchestra. Phil is certainly some little fiddler."

Taking Muriel by the arm, Jerry marched her up to Phyllis, who, with the other members of the orchestra, were also coming in for adulation. The addition of Jerry and Muriel to the group was soon noticeable by the burst of laughter which ascended therefrom. Good-natured Jerry had not the remotest idea of how very popular she really was.

Promptly on the heels of the stunt party followed a collation served in the dining room. An extra table had been added to the two long ones used by the residents. When the company trooped into the prettily-decorated room with its flower-trimmed tables, the Wayland Hall girls were pleasantly surprised to see Signor Baretti in charge there. While he had repeatedly refused at various times to cater for private parties given at the campus houses, Elaine had secured his valued services without much coaxing. He had long regarded her as "one the nicest, maybe the best, all my young ladies from the college."

It was one minute past eleven when the guests

rose from the table after a vigorous response to Portia's toast to Elaine, and joined in singing one stanza of "Auld Lang Syne." With the last note of the song hasty goodnights were said. "Not one minute later than half-past eleven" had been the stipulation laid down with the permission for the extra hour.

"We'll have to walk as though we all wore seven league boots," declared Jerry, as the Wayland Hall girls hurried down the steps of Silverton Hall. "But, oh, my goodness me, haven't we had a fine time? Tonight was like our good old Sanford crowd parties at home, wasn't it? It looks to me as though the right kind of times had actually struck Hamilton!"

CHAPTER IX

HER "DEAREST" WISH

IT did not need Elaine's party to cement more securely the friendship which existed between the Silvertonites and the group of Wayland Hallites who had co-operated with them so loyally from the first. They had fought side by side for principle. Now they were beginning to glimpse the lighter, happier side of affairs and experience the pleasure

of discovering how much each group had to admire
in the other.

"What we ought to do is organize a bureau of
entertainment and give musicales, plays, revues and
one thing or another," Robin proposed to Marjorie
as the two were returning from a trip to the town
of Hamilton one afternoon in early October. "We
would charge an admission fee, of course, and put
the money to some good purpose. I don't know
what we would do with it. There are so few really
needy students here. We'd find some worthy way
of spending it. I know we would make a lot. The
students simply mob the gym when there's a basket-ball game. They'd be willing to part with their
shekels for the kind of show we could give."

"I think the same," Marjorie made hearty response. "At home we gave a Campfire once, at
Thanksgiving. We held it in the armory. We
had booths and sold different things. We had a
show, too. That was the time Ronny danced those
two interpretative dances I told you of the other
night. We made over a thousand dollars. Half of
it went to the Sanford guards and the Lookouts
got the other half."

"We could make a couple of hundred dollars at
one revue, I believe. We could give about three
entertainments this year and three or four next,"
planned Robin. "It would have to be a fund de-

voted to helping the students, I guess. Come to think of it, I would not care to get up a show unless our purpose was clearly stated in the beginning. A few unjust persons might start the story that we wanted the money for ourselves. By the way, the Sans are not interesting themselves in our affairs this year, are they? Do you ever clash with them at the Hall?"

"No; they never notice us and we never notice them. It isn't much different in that respect than it was in the beginning. I'd feel rather queer about it sometimes if they hadn't been so utterly heartless in so many ways. This is their last year. It will seem queer when we come back next fall as seniors to have almost an entirely new set of girls in the house. I can't bear to think of losing Leila and Vera and Helen. Then there are Rosalind, Nella, Martha and Hortense; splendid girls, all of them. I wish they had been freshies with us. That's the beauty of the Silvertonites. They will all be graduated together."

"We are fortunate. Think of poor Phil! She is going to be lonesome when we all leave the good old port of Hamilton. To go back to the show idea. I'm going to talk it over with my old standbys at our house. You do the same at yours. Maybe some one of them will have a brilliant inspiration. I mean, about what we ought to do with the money, once we've made it."

A sudden jolt of the taxicab in which they were riding, as it swung to the right, combined with an indignant yell of protest from its driver, startled them both. A blue and buff car had shot past them, barely missing the side of the taxicab.

"Look where you're goin' or get off the road!" bawled the man after it. His face was scarlet with anger, he turned in his seat, addressing his fares. "That blue car near smashed us," he growled. "The young lady that drives it had better quit and give somebody else the wheel. This is the third time she near put my cab on the blink. She can't drive for sour apples. I wisht, if you knew her, you'd tell her she's gotta quit it. I don't own this cab. I don't wanta get mixed up in no smash-up. If she does it again I'll go up to the college boss and report that car."

"Neither of us know her well enough to give her your message," Marjorie smiled faintly, as she pictured herself giving the irate driver's warning to Elizabeth Walbert. She had recognized the girl at the wheel as the blue and buff car had passed her.

"I'll stop her myself and tell her where she gets off at," threatened the man. "I ain't afraida her."

"I think that would be a very good idea," calmly agreed Marjorie. "There is no reason why you should not rebuke her for her recklessness. She was at fault; not you."

"Do you imagine he really would report Miss Walbert to Doctor Matthews," inquired Robin in discreetly lowered tones, as the driver resumed attention at the wheel.

"He might. He would be more likely to do his talking to her," was Marjorie's opinion. "I tried to encourage him in that idea. A report of that kind to Dr. Matthews might result in the banning of cars at Hamilton."

"Did you hear last year, at the time Katherine was hurt, that Miss Cairns received a summons from Doctor Matthews? I was told that he gave her a severe lecture on reckless driving. She told some of the Sans and it came to Portia and I in a round-about way."

"I believe it to be true." Marjorie hesitated, then continued frankly. "Katherine did not report her."

Unbound by any promise of secrecy to any person, Marjorie acquainted Robin with the way the report of the accident had been put before the president. She and her chums had heard the story from Lillian Wenderblatt, who had so ardently urged her father to take up the cudgels for Katherine directly after the accident.

"Lillian explained to her father that Katherine

utterly refused to take the matter up. He reported it to the doctor of his own accord, saying that Katherine wished the affair closed. So Doctor Matthews didn't send for her at all. While he never referred to the subject afterward to Professor Wenderblatt, he said at the time of their talk that he would send Miss Cairns a summons to his office. Lillian's father said the doctor's word was equivalent to the summons. So I believe she received one. None of us who are Kathie's close friends ever mentioned it to others. Lillian told no one but us. She did not ask us to keep it a secret. We simply *did not talk* about it. That's why I felt free to tell you, since you asked me a direct question."

"Strange, isn't it, that the Sans can't even be loyal to one another," Robin commented. "Very likely Leslie Cairns told them in confidence, not expecting it would be betrayed. She may not know to this day that a girl of her own crowd told tales."

"She is not honorable herself. Her intimates know that." Marjorie's rejoinder held sternness. "There is nothing truer than the Bible verse: 'As ye sow, so must ye also reap.' She tries to gain whatever she happens to want by dishonorable methods. In turn, her chums behave dishonorably toward her.

"An unhappy state of affairs." Robin shrugged her disfavor. "Phil says Miss Walbert is a talker;

that she is becoming unpopular with the sophs who voted for her last year because she gossips."

Marjorie smiled whimsically. "Wouldn't it be poetic justice if she were to turn the half of her class who were for her last year against her by her own unworthiness? After Miss Cairns worked so hard to establish her too! There's surely a greater inclination toward democracy than last year, or Phil wouldn't have won the sophomore presidency."

"Yes; and she won it by eighteen votes this year over Miss Keene, and she is one of Miss Walbert's pals. Last year she lost it by nine. Some difference!" Robin looked her pride of her lovable cousin. "I think there is a great change for the better in Hamilton since we were freshies, don't you?"

Marjorie made quick assent. "You Silverites have done the most for Hamilton," she commended. "We Lookouts have tried our hardest, but we couldn't have done much if you hadn't been behind us like a solid wall."

"You Lookouts deserve as much credit as we. You girls are social successes in the nicest way, because you have all been so friendly and sweet to everyone. Then you have fought shoulder to shoulder with us. Now that we have begun to make our influence felt, we should follow it up by giving entertainments in which the whole college can have a part."

"Let's do this," Marjorie proposed. "Bring the orchestra and Hope Morris, she's so nice, over to Wayland Hall on Saturday evening. I'll have a spread. Then we can plan something to give in the near future. Here's my getting-off place. Goodbye."

The taxicab having reached a point on the main campus drive where two other drives branched off right and left, the machine slowed down. She rarely troubled the driver to take her to the door of the Hall, it being but a few rods distant from this point.

Swinging up the drive and into the Hall in her usual energetic fashion, Marjorie's first move was toward the bulletin board. Three letters was the delightful harvest she reaped from it. One in Constance's small fine hand, one from General. The third she eyed rather suspiciously. It was in an unfamiliar hand and bore the address, "Marjorie Dean, Hamilton College."

"An advertisement, I guess," was her frowning reflection as she went on upstairs. "Anyone I know, well enough to receive a letter from, would know my house address."

Anxious to relieve her arms of several bundles containing purchases made at Hamilton before opening her letters, Marjorie did not stop to examine her mail on the landing. Entering her room, she found it deserted of Jerry's always congenial company. Immediately she dropped her packages on the center table and plumped down to enjoy her letters.

Second glance at the letter informed her that the envelope was of fine expensive paper. This fact dismissed the advertisement idea. Marjorie toyed with it rather nervously. In the past she had received enough annoying letters to make her dread the sight of her address in unfamiliar handwriting. On the verge of reveling in the other two whose contents she was sure to love, she hated the idea of a disagreeable shock. She knew of no reason why she should be the recipient of any such letter. That, however, would not prevent an unworthy person from writing one.

Determined to read it first and have it over with, Marjorie tore open an end of the envelope and extracted the missive from it. A hasty glance at the end and she vented a relieved "A-h-h!" Turning back to the beginning, she read with rising color:

"MARJORIE DEAN,
    Hamilton College.
"DEAR CHILD:

"Will you come to Hamilton Arms to tea next Thursday afternoon at five o'clock? I find I have

the wish to see and talk with you again. I prefer
you to keep the matter of your visit from your girl
friends. I am not on good terms with Hamilton
College and its students, and the information that
I had invited you to tea would form a choice bit of
campus gossip.

> "Yours sincerely,
>> "SUSANNA CRAIG HAMILTON."

CHAPTER X

HAMILTON ARMS AND ITS OWNER

"WELL, of all things!" Marjorie could not get
over her undiluted amazement. For a second it
struck her that she might again be the victim of a
hoax. Perhaps an unkindly-minded person wished
her to essay a call on Miss Susanna, thinking she
might receive a sound snubbing. She shook her
head at this canny suspicion. The phrasing was
unmistakably Miss Susanna's. She doubted also
whether anyone had seen her that day with the old
lady. Only a few cars had passed them before they
had turned into the private road. These had contained persons not from the college. Outside the
Lookouts, only Katherine, Leila and Vera knew of

her encounter with Miss Susanna. She had not thought of keeping it a secret. She now made mental note to tell the girls not to mention it to anyone.

This resolve brought with it the annoying cogigation that the girls would wonder why she suddenly wished the matter kept secret. Nor could she explain to them without violating Miss Hamilton's request. She could readily understand the latter's point of view. Miss Susanna could not be blamed for taking it. Marjorie could only wish the old lady knew how honorable and discreet her chums were. She decided she would endeavor to make her hostess acquainted with that truth during her call.

She came to the conclusion that she could not pledge her close friends to secrecy regarding her recent adventure until after she had been to Hamilton Arms and talked with its eccentric owner. Miss Susanna would no doubt be displeased to learn that she had already mentioned their meeting to others. She would have to be told of it, nevertheless.

Marjorie's next problem was to slip quietly away on Thursday afternoon without saying where she was going. That would not be difficult, provided none of the Lookouts happened to desire her company on some particular jaunt or merry-making. An indefinite refusal on her part would bring down on her a volley of mischievous questions.

"I'll have to keep clear of the girls on Thursday," she ruminated, with a half vexed smile. "I'll have to put on the gown I'm going to wear to tea in the morning and wear it all day so as not to arouse their curiosity. That's a nuisance. I'd like to wear one of my best frocks and I can't on account of chemistry. I'll wear that organdie frock Jerry likes so much; the one with the yellow rosebud in it. It is not fussy. If it is cold or rainy I can wear a long coat over it. I hope it's a nice day. I can wear my picture hat. It goes so well with that gown. I can slip it out of the Hall without them noticing if I swing it on my arm. I hope to goodness I don't ruin my organdie during chemistry. I feel like a conspirator."

Marjorie chuckled faintly as she rose from her chair, letter in hand. She tucked the letter away in the top drawer of her chiffonier with the optimistic opinion that it would not be very long before she could frankly tell her chums of its contents.

Fortune favored her on Thursday. She awoke with a stream of brilliant sunshine in her face. She rejoiced that the day was fair and hoped Miss Susanna would suggest a walk about the grounds. Then she remembered the request the latter had made, and smiled at her own stupidity. A walk about the grounds would probably be the last thing Miss Susanna would suggest.

As it happened, Jerry had made an engagement to go to Hamilton with Helen. Ronny had a theme in French to write, which she said would take her spare time both in the afternoon and evening. Lucy and Katherine would be in the Biological Laboratory until dinner time, and Leila and Vera were invited to a tea given by a senior to ten of her classmates. These were the only ones to be directly interested in her movements. To Jerry's invitation, "Want to go to town with Helen and I this afternoon?" she had replied, "No, Jeremiah," in as casual a tone as she could command, and that had ended the matter.

Marjorie was doubly careful in the Chemical Laboratory that afternoon and walked from it this time with no disfiguring stains on her dainty organdie frock. The letter had named the hour for her visit as five o'clock. This gave her ample time to return to the Hall, re-coif her curly hair and add a pretty satin sash of wide pale yellow ribbon to her costume. The absence of Jerry was, for once, welcome. She had a free hand to put the finishing touches to her toilet. It appealed to a certain sense of dignity, latent within her, to be able to quietly adjust her hat before the mirror and walk openly out of Wayland Hall. Marjorie inwardly hated anything connected with secrecy, yet it seemed to her she was always becoming involved in something which demanded it.

When finally she emerged from the Hall, she did not follow the main drive but cut across the campus, making for the western entrance. Reaching the highway, she kept a sharp lookout for passing automobiles. She laughed to herself as she thought of how disconcerting it would be after all her pains to run squarely into Jerry and Helen. The latter had just been the lucky recipient of a limousine, long promised her by her father, and she and Jerry were trying it out that afternoon.

It was ten minutes to five when, without having met anyone save two or three campus acquaintances, Marjorie walked sedately between the high, ornamental gate posts of Hamilton Arms, and on up the drive to the house. She compared her present approach to that of last May Day evening, when she had stolen like a shadow to the veranda to hang the May basket. It did not seem quite real to her that now she was actually coming to Hamilton Arms as an invited guest.

The knocker was no easier to pull than it had been on that night. She waited, feeling as though she were about to leave the college world behind and enter one rich in the romance of Colonial days. Then the door opened slowly and a dignified old man with thick, snow-white hair and a smooth-shaven face stood regarding her solemnly.

"You are Marjorie Dean?" he interrogated in deep, but very gentle tones. This before she had time to ask for Miss Susanna.

"Yes," she affirmed, smiling in her unaffected, charming fashion. "I—Miss Hamilton expects me to tea."

"I know." He bowed with grave politeness. "Come in. Miss Susanna is in the library. I will show you the way."

Marjorie drew a long breath of admiration as she was ushered into a wide almost square reception hall paneled in walnut. Her feet sank deep into the heavy brown velvet rug which completely covered the floor. Walking quickly behind her guide, she had no more than time for a passing glance at the massive elegance of the carved walnut furniture. She caught a fleeting glimpse of herself in the great square mirror of the hall rack and thought how very small and insignificant she appeared.

"How are you, Marjorie Dean?" Ushered into the library by the stately old man, the last of the Hamiltons now came forward to greet her.

"I am very well, thank you. I hope you are feeling well, too, Miss Susanna."

Marjorie took the small, sturdy hand Miss Susanna extended in both her own. The mistress of Hamilton Arms looked so very tiny in the great room. Marjorie experienced a wave of sudden tenderness for her.

"Yes; I am well, by the grace of God and my own good sense," returned her hostess in her brisk, almost hard tones. "You are prompt to the hour, child. I like that. I hate to be kept waiting. I have my tea at precisely five o'clock. It is years since I had a guest to tea. Sit down there." She indicated a straight chair with an ornamental leather back and seat. Jonas will bring the tea table in directly, and serve the tea. Take off your hat and lay it on the library table. I wish to see you without it."

She had not more than finished speaking, when the snowy-haired servitor wheeled in a good-sized rosewood tea-table. He drew it up to where Marjorie sat, and brought another chair for the mistress of Hamilton Arms similar to the one on which the guest was sitting. Withdrawing from the room, he left youth and age to take tea together.

"Who would have thought that I should ever pour tea for one of my particular aversions," Miss Susanna commented with grim humor. "Do you take sugar and cream, child?"

"Two lumps of sugar and no cream." Marjorie held out her hand for the delicate Sevres cup.

"Help yourself to the muffins and jam. It is red

raspberry. I put it up myself. Now eat as though you were hungry. I am always ravenous for my tea. I do not have dinner until eight and I am outdoors so much I grow very hungry as five o'clock approaches."

"I am awfully hungry," Marjorie confessed. "I love five o'clock tea. We have it at home in summer but not in winter. We girls at Hamilton hardly ever have it, because we have dinner shortly after six."

"At what campus house are you?" was the abrupt question.

"Wayland Hall. I like it best of all, though Silverton Hall is a fine house."

"Wayland Hall," the old lady repeated. "It was his favorite house."

"You are speaking of Mr. Brooke Hamilton?" Marjorie inquired with breathless interest. "Miss Remson said it was his favorite house. He was so wonderful. 'We shall ne'er see his like again,' " she quoted, her brown eyes eloquent.

Miss Susanna stared at her in silence, as though trying to determine the worth of Marjorie's unexpected remarks.

"He *was* wonderful," she said at last. "I am amazed at your appreciation of him. You *are* an amazing young person, I must say. How much do you know concerning my great uncle that you should have arrived at your truly high opinion of him?"

"I know very little about him except that he loved Hamilton and planned it nobly." Marjorie's clear eyes looked straight into her vis-a-vis's sharp dark ones. "I have asked questions. I have treasured every scrap of information about him that I have heard since I came to Hamilton College. No one seems to know much of him except in a general way."

"That is true. Well, the fault lies with the college." The reply hinted of hostility. "Perhaps I will tell you more of him some day. Not now; I am not in the humor. I must get used to having you here first. I try to forget that you are from the college. I told you I did not like girls. I may call you an exception, child. I realized that after you had left me, the day you helped me to the cottage with the chrysanthemums. I was cheered by your company. I am pleased with your admiration for him. He was worthy of it."

As on the day of her initial meeting with Brooke Hamilton's great niece, Marjorie was again at a loss as to what to say next. She wished to say how greatly she revered the memory of the founder of Hamilton College. In the face of Miss Susanna's declaration that she did not wish to talk of him, she could not frame a reply that conveyed her reverence.

"Try these cakes. They are from an old recipé the Hamiltons have used for four generations. Ellen, my cook, made these. I seldom do any baking now. I used to when younger. I spend most of my time out of doors in good weather. Let me have your cup."

Her hostess tendered a plate of delicate little cakes not unlike macaroons. Marjorie helped herself to the cakes and forebore asking questions about Brooke Hamilton. Miss Susanna had partially promised to tell her of him some day. She could do no more than possess her soul in patience.

"What do you do in winter, Miss Hamilton, when you can't be out?" she questioned interestedly. "Do you live at Hamilton Arms the year round?"

"Yes; I have not been away from here for a number of years. In winter I read and embroider. I do plain sewing for the poor of Hamilton. Jonas takes baskets of clothing and necessities to needy families in the town of Hamilton. 'The poor ye have always with ye,' you know."

"I know," Marjorie affirmed, her lovely face growing momently sad. "Captain, I mean, my mother, does a good deal of such work in Sanford. I have helped her a little. During our last year at high school a number of us organized a club. We called ourselves the Lookouts and we rented a house and started a day nursery for the mill children. The house was in their district."

"And how long did you keep it up?" was the somewhat skeptical inquiry.

"Oh, it is running along beautifully yet." Marjorie laughed as she made answer.

"I am more amazed than before. A club of girls usually hangs together about six weeks. Each girl feels that she ought to be at the head of it and in the end a grand falling-out occurs." Miss Susanna's eyes were twinkling. This time her remarks were not pointedly ill-natured. "You are to tell me about this club," she commanded.

Marjorie complied, giving her a brief history of the day nursery.

"Are any of your Lookouts here at Hamilton with you?" she was interrogated.

"Four of them. One, Lucy Warner, won a scholarship to Hamilton." Now on the subject, Marjorie determined to make a valiant stand for her chums. She therefore told of the offering of the scholarship by Ronny and of Lucy's brilliancy as a student. She told of Lucy's ability as a secretary and of how much she had done to help herself through college. She did not forget to speak of Katherine Langly, and her exceptional winning of a scholarship especially offered by Brooke Hamilton.

"I had no idea there were any such girls over there." The old lady spoke half to herself. "I might have known there would be some apostles."

"Miss Susanna,"— Marjorie decided that this would be the best time to acquaint her hostess with what she had purposed to tell her,—"I told my intimate friends of meeting you the day the basket handle broke. I thought you ought to know that. You had asked me in your letter not to mention to anyone that I was coming here. I did not say a word to anyone of the letter. I would ask my chums not to mention what I told them about meeting you in the first place, but, if I do, they will wish to know why."

"Humph!" The listener used Jerry's pet interjection. "Where did you tell them you were going today? Some of them must have seen you as you came away."

"No; they were all out except one girl. She was busy writing a theme."

"What would you have told them if they had seen you?" Miss Hamilton eyed the young girl searchingly.

"I would have said I was going out and hoped they wouldn't feel hurt if I didn't tell them my destination. What else could I have said?" It was

Marjorie's turn to fix her gaze upon her hostess.

"Nothing else, by rights. If I allowed you to tell your chums, as you call them, that you were here today, would they keep your counsel? How many of them would have to know it?" The older woman's face had softened wonderfully.

Marjorie thought for an instant. "Eight," she answered. "They are honorable. I would like to tell them."

"Very well, you may." The permission came concisely. "I will take your word for their discretion. I have my own proper reasons for not wishing to be gossiped about on the campus. I wish you to come again. I do not wish your visits to be a secret. I abhor that kind of secrecy. Perhaps in time I shall not care if the whole college knows. At present what they do not know will not hurt them. In the words of my distinguished uncle, 'Be not secret; be discreet.'"

CHAPTER XI

COMPARING NOTES

TEA over, Jonas removed the tea-table and Miss Susanna waved her guest toward a leather-covered arm chair. Changing her own chair for one corresponding to Marjorie's, Miss Hamilton proceeded to ply Marjorie with interested questions concerning her college course. She exhibited a kind of repressed eagerness to hear of the college and her guest's doings there.

The tall rosewood floor clock had chimed six, then again the musical stroke of half hour, before Marjorie found graceful opportunity to take her leave. She was willing to stay longer, but was not certain that her erratic hostess would wish her to do so. The shadows had begun to fall across the sombre elegance of the library and the October twilight would soon be upon them.

Miss Susanna made no effort to detain her beyond saying: "So you think you must go. Well, you will be coming again soon to see me. You have given me much to think of." She accom-

panied Marjorie to the front door, giving her a
warm handshake in parting. Marjorie noticed,
however, that her small face wore a pensive expression quite at variance with her accustomed alert
demeanor. It gave her the appearance of great age,
though her brown hair was only partially streaked
with gray. Marjorie thought she could not be
much more than sixty years old.

A happy little smile touched the pleased lieutenant's lips as she hurried toward the campus
through the gathering twilight. Far from being
dissatisfied at not hearing more of Brooke Hamilton, she was blissfully content with her visit. Miss
Susanna had promised to tell her of him. She had
given her consent to allowing Marjorie to inform
her chums of her visit to Hamilton Arms. She had
actually set foot in the house of her dreams. The
two rooms she had seen had more than justified her
expectations of what it would be like inside.

Dinner was on when she reached Wayland Hall.
Marjorie had fared too well on hot muffins, jam,
cakes, and the most delicious tea she had ever
drunk, to care for anything more to eat.

"Where, may I ask, have you been keeping yourself?" saluted Jerry about twenty minutes after
Marjorie's return. Coming into their room she
beheld her missing room-mate calmly preparing her

French lesson for the next day. "Why don't you go and have your dinner? Or have you had it?"

"I have had tea instead of dinner. I couldn't eat another mouthful to save me. 'An' ye hae been where I hae been,'" hummed Marjorie mischievously.

"Something like that," satirized Jerry. "Where did you say you were? Never mind. I am sure you will tell me some day." She simpered at Marjorie. "You should have been with Helen and I today. Something awfully funny happened. Not to us. The girls are coming up to hear about it soon. Helen and I didn't care to tell it at the table on account of the Sans."

"Then farewell to my peaceful study hour." Marjorie laid away the translation she had been making.

"You can chase the girls away at eight-thirty, that will give you time enough. If you don't, I will. I have studying of my own to do."

"As long as the gang will be here I may as well save *my* remarks until then."

A buzz of voices outside the door announced the "gang." Beside the three Lookouts and Katherine were the beloved trio, Helen, Leila and Vera. The entire crowd pounced upon Marjorie, demanding to know where she had been. It was unusual for her to be away without having left word with some one of them.

"Will I tell you where I was? Certainly! It's no secret; at least not now," she added tantalizingly. "Don't you want to hear Jerry's tale first? I do."

"Nothing doing. You go ahead and relieve our anxious minds. We didn't know but maybe you had been spirited away by a bogus note again."

A peculiar expression appeared in Marjorie's eyes as she went to her chiffonier and drew from it Miss Hamilton's letter.

"It's queer, but when I received this letter the other day, I was almost afraid it was another fake. Notice the address, then read it," she commanded, handing it to Vera who was nearest her.

It brought forth exclamatory comment from all, once each had acquainted herself with its contents.

"No wonder you didn't leave word where you were going. Did you have a nice time?" Jerry's chubby features registered her pleasure of the honor accorded her room-mate.

"Yes; I had a beautiful time. I was worried because I couldn't speak of going to any of you. Miss Susanna gave me permission to tell you eight, but no others." Marjorie recounted her visit in detail. "I wish she would invite the rest of you to Hamilton Arms. It is a beautiful house inside. I

only saw the hall and library, but they were magnificent."

"Don't weep, Marvelous Manager." Ronny had
noted Marjorie's wistful expression. "Through
your miraculous machinations we shall all be parading about Hamilton Arms in the near future."

"I certainly hope so," was the fervent response.

For a little the bevy of girls discussed Marjorie's
news. All were elated over the pleasure which had
come to her. Her generous thought of the peculiar
old lady on May Day of the previous year had
touched them.

"She hasn't asked you yet if you hung that basket, has she?" queried Lucy.

"How could she possibly suspect me of hanging
it?" laughed Marjorie.

"Because it was like you. It carried your atmos-
phere. Some day she will suddenly notice that and
ask you about the basket," Lucy sagely prophesied.
"She seems to be a shrewd old person."

"She is." Marjorie smiled at the candid criti-
cism. She wondered if Miss Susanna had not been
in her youth a trifle like Lucy.

"Now for what Helen and I saw and heard this
afternoon," declared Jerry gleefully. The first interest in Marjorie's visit to Hamilton Arms had
abated.

"Oh, a horrible tale I have to tell,
   Of the terrible fate that once befell
   A couple of students who resided
   In the very same neighborhood that I did,"

chanted Helen. "You tell it, Jeremiah. You can make it funnier than I can."

"Helen and I started out with the new car as proudly as you please this afternoon," began Jerry with a reminiscent chuckle. "We hadn't gone much further than Hamilton Arms when whiz, bing, buzz! Along came that Miss Walbert in her blue and buff car and nearly bumped into us. She came up from behind and her car just missed scraping against Helen's. Leslie Cairns was with her. We never said a word, but I heard Miss Cairns raise her voice. I think she gave Miss Walbert a call down."

"There was no excuse for her, except that she never seems to pay any particular attention to anyone's car but her own," put in Helen. "I have heard complaint of her from I don't remember how many girls who own cars. Occasionally you will find a girl who can't learn to drive a car. She belongs in that class. Excuse me for butting in. Proceed, Jeremiah."

"That's all of the prologue," Jerry continued. "Now comes the first act. We went on to town, drove around a little, did our errands, had ice cream at the Lotus and started back highly pleased with ourselves. You know that place just before you leave the town where the turn into Hamilton Highway is made? There is a grocery store and a garage on one side of the road and a hotel on the other. Just before we came to that point Miss Walbert and her car whizzed by us again. She took that corner with a lurch. When we struck the place a minute later we saw something had happened. She had actually scraped the side of one of those taxis that run between town and the college. It was coming from the college, I suppose. Anyway, Miss Cairns and she were both out of their car and so was the taxi driver. Maybe he wasn't giving those two a call down!"

Jerry and Helen exchanged joyful smiles at the recollection of the reckless couple's discomfiture.

"Helen drove very slowly past them. We wanted to hear what the man was saying," Jerry continued. "He was laying down the law to them to beat the band. We heard Leslie Cairns say, 'Do you know to whom you are talking?' He shouted out, 'Yes; to a simpleton of a girl who don't know no more about drivin' than a goose. I seen you drive your own car, lady, an' I never had no trouble with you. Your friend, there, is the limit. You're runnin' chances of landin' in the hospital or worse when

you go ridin' with her.' Leslie Cairns was furious.
I could tell that by her expression. Miss Walbert
fairly shrieked something at him. She was mad as
hops, too. We had passed them by that time so we
couldn't catch what she was saying. There was
quite a crowd around them, mostly men and young-
sters."

"That must be the man Robin and I rode with
the other day," Marjorie said. "Is he short, with
a red face and quite gray hair?"

"Yes; that's the man. How did you know which
one it was?" Jerry showed surprise.

"He had a near collision with Miss Walbert that
day." Marjorie related the incident.

"It is a shame!" Leila's face had darkened as
she listened to both girls. "I hope Leslie Cairns
takes her in hand. She's the very one to cause a
bad accident and then home go our cars. She is
such a poor driver. She bowls along the road without regard for man or beast. She has a good car
which will presently be in the ditch."

"Do you think President Matthews would ban
cars if a Hamilton girl were to ditch her car or met
with serious accident to herself?" Vera asked re-
flectively.

"Hard to say, Midget. It would depend upon
the seriousness of the accident. Suppose a girl
were to ditch her car and be killed. It would be

horrifying. I doubt whether we would be allowed
our cars after any such accident."

"Grant nothing like that ever happens." Lucy
Warner gave a slight shudder. "I shall never forget the day Kathie was hurt."

"None of us who were with her that day are
likely ever to forget it. Miss Cairns escaped easily
considering the way she was driving. She ought to
be the very one to tell that Miss Walbert a few
things not in the automobile guide," declared Jerry.
"She certainly did not appear at advantage this
afternoon."

CHAPTER XII

A TRAITOR IN CAMP

LESLIE CAIRNS' opinion of the matter coincided
with Jerry's, though the latter could not know it.
To become involved in a roadside argument with an
irate taxicab driver did not appeal to her in the
least. She was not half so angry with him, however, as with Elizabeth Walbert. She blamed the
latter for the whole thing. For several minutes
after Helen and Jerry had driven by them, Elizabeth and the driver continued to quarrel.

"How much do you want for the damage you

say we have done your cab?" Leslie had impatiently inquired of the man. "Cut it out, Bess, and get back to your car," she had ordered in the next breath. "Let me settle this business."

A momentary hesitation and Elizabeth had obeyed. She could not afford to antagonize Leslie, at present. She had an axe of her own yet to be ground.

"I oughtta have twenty-five dollars. It ain't my car. Repairin' comes high."

"Very good. Here is your money. Wait a minute." Leslie had extracted the sum from her handbag. With it came a small pad of blank paper and a fountain pen. Then and there she obtained not only a receipt for the money but a statement of release as well. She was well aware that it would not cost twenty-five dollars to repaint the side of the cab scraped by their car, but she preferred the matter summarily closed.

Returning to the car she had said shortly: "I'll take the wheel." Elizabeth had resumed the driver's seat. Nor had she made any move toward relinquishing it.

"You heard what I said, Bess," she had sharply rebuked. "Either that, or you and I are on the outs for good. You let me drive that car and show you a few things you need badly to know about driving." Leslie's lowering face and tense utterance had had its effect. Elizabeth had allowed her to drive back to Hamilton but had sulked all the way to the campus.

At the garage she had unbent a little and inquired how much Leslie had paid the driver. "I'll return it to you next week," she had promised.

"Suit yourself about that. I'm in no hurry. I took it upon myself to settle with the idiot. It wouldn't worry me if you never paid it. I thought it best to pacify him. I don't care to have him reporting us to Matthews as he threatened to do." This had been Leslie's mind on the subject.

"I don't believe he would ever go near Doctor Matthews. Still *you* couldn't afford to risk being reported," Elizabeth had retorted with special emphasis on the "you."

To this Leslie had vouchsafed no reply. She had merely stared at her companion in a most disconcerting fashion and walked off and left her. She was thoroughly nettled with Elizabeth for her lack of gratitude. Natalie was right about her it seemed. She was also wondering where the ungrateful sophomore had obtained certain information which she apparently possessed. No one beyond her seven intimates among the Sans knew that she had been reprimanded by President Matthews for the accident to Katherine Langly. To the other members

of the club she had intimated that she had adjusted
the matter quietly with Katherine.

That evening, while Jerry was recounting to her
chums what she and Helen had heard of the altercation between the cab driver and the two girls,
Leslie was having a confidential talk with Natalie
Weyman. She had gone straight from the garage
to her room, eaten dinner at the Hall and asked
Natalie to come to her room after dinner.

"Nat, you are right about Bess. She is no
good," Leslie began, dropping into a chair opposite
that of her friend. Briefly narrating the happening
of the afternoon, she repeated the remark Elizabeth
had made to her at the garage. "What would you
draw from that?" she asked.

"Someone has been talking." Natalie compressed
her lips in a tight line. "You are sure you never
told her yourself?"

"*Positively, no*. I have never babbled my private
affairs to Bess, or Lola either. Only the old crowd
were told the facts of that trouble. We have a
traitor in the camp and *I know who it is*." Leslie's
eyes narrowed with sinister significance. It's Dulcie. I am going to find out quietly what all she
has been saying about me and to whom she has been
saying it. I'm sure she told Bess about the summons. That isn't so serious. I could overlook that,
although I don't like it. It is the other things she

may have told. That's what worries me. She and
I have been on the outs since that Valentine masquerade last year. She hardly ever comes to my
room. I am not sorry. I never got along well with
Dulcie. I never trusted her."

"Dulcie ought to know better than tell all she
knows to that Walbert creature," Natalie made indignant return. "Why, Les, suppose she were foolish enough to tell her about that high tribunal
stunt?" Natalie drew a sharp breath of consternation. "Dulcie knows the rights of the Remson mix-
up, too."

"Dulcie knows too much. So do some of the
other girls. If I had it to do over again, I would
not tell anyone but you how I put over a stunt.
Why did we haze Bean? Simply because she reported me to Matthews after Langly had agreed to
drop it. The girls were all in on the hazing, so not
one of them would be safe if they told it."

"The Remson affair would do you the most harm
if it got out," Natalie said decidedly. "It is contemptible in Dulcie to gossip about you after all the
favors you have done her. You've lent her money
over and over again. You know she never pays it
back if she can slide out of it."

Leslie made an indifferent gesture of assent.
"She owes me over two hundred dollars now. I
lent it to her during her freshie year. She paid up

what she borrowed of me last year, but she never said a word about the other. Dulcie has *nerve*, Nat; pure, unadulterated *nerve*. She can't bear me lately because I run the Sans to suit myself. I always ran the club and she knows that. Last year she decided that she would like to run it herself. I sat down on her every time she tried it. She deliberately left the back door of that house unlocked the night we hazed Bean. I told her to see to it. She was edgeways at me. She never went near the door. You know what happened."

"Dulcie will have to be told a few plain truths." Natalie frowned displeased anxiety. The news of Dulcie's defection was rather alarming.

"She is going to hear them from me, but not yet. I shall catch her dead to rights before I have things out with her. I've made up my mind just how I am going to do it, provided the rest of the Sans stand by me. It will be to their interest to do so. I mean, with their support, I can give her precisely what she deserves."

"I'll stand by you. Joan will, too. She is down on Dulcie for some reason or other. They haven't been on speaking terms for a week. I asked Joan what the trouble was between them. She said Dulcie made her weary and she didn't care whether she ever spoke to her again or not. That was all I could get out of her."

"Hm-m!" Leslie looked interested. "I shall find out tomorrow what Joan has against her. If Dulcie hasn't gabbed anything worse to Bess, and I presume a few others, than the news that I received a summons from his high and cranky mightiness, I will let her off with my candid opinion of her. If she has been a busy little news distributor of secret matters, she will rue it. I'll have no traitors among the Sans."

CHAPTER XIII

WELL MATCHED

LESLIE'S first crafty move toward determining Dulcie Vale's treachery was in the direction of Elizabeth Walbert. The latter had promised to return the next week the twenty-five dollars Leslie had expended in her behalf. Leslie planned to wait until she did so before making an attempt to discover how many of the Sans' secrets Elizabeth knew. She was certain that Elizabeth would return the loan promptly, as she received a large allowance from home and as much more as she chose to demand.

To seek the self-satisfied sophomore's society was

not what Leslie proposed to do. She intended matters should be the other way around. She could
then take Elizabeth completely off her guard and
find out more easily what Dulcie had imparted to
her.

Elizabeth also had views of her own regarding
Leslie. The latter had not been nearly so friendly
with her since college had opened as she had been
during the previous year. Leslie had renewed her
old comradeship with Natalie Weyman, whom
Elizabeth detested and stood a little in fear of.
Natalie had never been friendly with her. She had
always held herself aloof. Whenever they chanced
to meet she treated Elizabeth as a mere acquaintance. It was galling to the ambitious, self-seeking
sophomore, but she loftily ignored Natalie's frigid-
ity. She had complained of it once to Leslie and
been soundly snubbed for her pains. "You needn't
expect much of Nat. She doesn't like you. That's
why she freezes you out. It won't do you any good
to tell me about it, for Nat is my particular pal."
This had been Leslie's unsympathetic reception of
the complaint.

In her heart Elizabeth did not like Leslie. She
resented Leslie's domineering ways. This did not
deter her from fawning upon the despotic senior.
She was depending on Leslie to help her regain a
certain popularity which had been hers as a fresh-

man. She had cherished a vain hope that she might be elected to the sophomore presidency. To her chagrin she had not even been nominated. Determined to shine on the campus, her thoughts were now turning toward basket ball. She was now anxious to enlist Leslie's services in helping her devise a means of making the sophomore team. As a senior Leslie could easily influence the sports committee to favor her. Mae Lowry and Sarah Pierce, both Sans, were on the committee.

It had been rumored that Professor Leonard and the sports committee had disagreed; that the instructor had coolly advised the committee to do as it pleased and dropped all interest in sports for that year. With him out of the reckoning, nothing stood in her way provided Leslie chose to favor her.

Her greatest ambition, however, was to belong to the Sans. She was always privately wishing that one member of the club would drop out. Leslie had once more told her that the club limit was eighteen members. If anyone left the club an outside eligible would be chosen to replace the retiring member so as to keep the number of girls at eighteen. She had also tried on the previous June to arrange for a room at Wayland Hall for the ensuing college year. She had been unsuccessful in the attempt.

After leaving Leslie on the occasion of her mishap on Hamilton Highway, she had realized her folly in showing spleen against her companion. She resolved to offset it as speedily as possible. She wrote Leslie a note which remained unanswered. She then telephoned the Hall, but Leslie was out. Her allowance check having arrived, she had an excuse to go to see Leslie. Her afternoon classes over, she set out for Wayland Hall one rainy afternoon, hoping the inclement weather had kept Leslie indoors.

Her baby-blue eyes gleamed triumph at the cheering news that Miss Cairns was in. As she ascended the stairs to Leslie's room, which was the largest and most expensive in the house, her curious glances roved everywhere. She wished she could see into the room of every student. Her lips fell into an envious pout as she thought of her own failure to get into the Hall. She would try again in June, on that she was determined.

Coming to the door of Leslie's room, she uttered a muffled exclamation of impatience. A large "Busy" sign stared her in the face. She did not turn and go away. Instead her surveying eyes took in the long hall from end to end. Next, she drew close to the door and listened. She could hear no voices from within. Leslie was evidently alone and studying.

With a defiant lifting of her chin Elizabeth

rapped on the panel twice and loudly. She listened again and was repaid by the sound of a chair being hastily moved, then approaching footsteps. The door opened with a jerk. Leslie stared at her visitor with no pleasantness.

"I came to return that twenty-five dollars." Elizabeth did not give Leslie a chance to speak first. "I saw the sign on your door. I thought I would knock, anyway. I've been trying to see you for a week to give it to you. Why didn't you answer my note, or didn't you receive it?"

Leslie continued to stare. She was taken aback for an instant by the cool impudence of the other girl. This was in reality the only thing about Elizabeth that Leslie liked. She found the sophomore's bold assurance amusing.

"Come in," she drawled, assuming her most indifferent pose. "I intended asking you if you could read. I'll forgive you. I told you there was no hurry about that money."

"What's money to me? Not that much!" Elizabeth snapped her fingers. "I can have all the money I want to spend here. I simply happened to be without it the other day. I won't stay. I see you are really busy writing letters. It goes to show you can write. I thought perhaps you had forgotten how."

Having delivered this thrust she busied herself

with her handbag. "Here you are; much obliged."
She tendered the money to Leslie. "I must go."
She turned as though to depart.

"Oh, sit down!" Leslie tossed the little wad of
bills on the table. "I can finish this letter later. I
have to keep that sign on the door when I want to
be alone. I'd be mobbed if I did not."

At heart Leslie was distinctly glad to see her
caller. She had her part to play on the stage of
deceit, however.

"I suppose the Sans are running in and out of
your room a good deal," Elizabeth returned enviously. "I wish I could live here. It makes me so
cross when I think of that Miss Dean and those
girls living here and I can't get in. There will be
a lot of girls graduated from here in June. I think
I can make it next fall. What's the use, though.
You'll be gone. It is on your account I'd like to be
here. I think more of you, Leslie, than of all the
rest of the girls put together." Elizabeth simulated wistful regret. She had tried out that particular expression before the mirror until she had per-
fected it. It was useful on so many occasions.

"Do you truly think as much of me as you say,
Bess, or are you simply talking to hear yourself
talk?" Leslie carried out admirably a pretense of
sudden earnestness.

"Why, *of course,* I care a lot about you, Leslie."

Elizabeth adopted a slightly grieved tone. "Think of how *much* you have done for me."

"Oh, that's all right." Leslie dismissed the reminder with a wave of the hand. "I have a reason for asking you that question. I have one or two other questions to ask you, too. If you are my friend, *and wish to continue to be my friend,* you will answer them."

"I certainly will, if I can," was the glib promise.

"You can," Leslie curtly assured. First, who told you about my having received a summons to Matthews' office on account of that accident to Langly last fall?"

"How do you know——" began the sophomore, then bit her lip.

"I *know.* There isn't much goes on on the campus that I don't know." This with intent to intimidate. "I know who told you, for that matter."

"I promised I wouldn't tell. Still, if you say you know who it was, I believe you do." Elizabeth hastily conceded, remembering her own interests. "You won't let on that I told you?"

Leslie shook her head. "Trust me to be discreet," she said.

"It was Dulcie Vale," came the treacherous answer.

"I knew it." Leslie brought one hand sharply

down against the other. "What else has Dulcie told you?"

"About what?" counter-questioned the sophomore.

"That's what I am asking you." Leslie leaned forward in her chair, steady eyes on her vis-a-vis.

Elizabeth experienced inward trepidation. Dulcie had told her a great many things which she had promptly repeated to friends of hers under promise of secrecy. Suppose Leslie had traced some bit of gossip to her. She had heard that Leslie could pretend affability when she was the angriest. She might be only using Dulcie as a blind in order to extract a confession from her.

"I don't quite understand you, Leslie," she asserted, knitting her light brows. "Dulcie has talked to me a little about the Sans. I never mentioned a word she said to anyone else."

"That's not the point. I am not accusing you of talking too much. You made a remark the other day which I took as an assumption that you had been told about the summons. I knew Dulcie had told you. Dulcie has said things to others, too."

"Oh, I know that." Confidence returning, Elizabeth was quick to place the blame on the absent Dulcie.

"Yes; and so do I. It is very necessary that I should get to the bottom of her talk. Some say one

thing about her, some another. I thought I could
rely on you for the facts."

"I don't care to have any trouble with Dulcie
over this," deprecated Elizabeth.

"You won't. Your name won't be mentioned in
it. All I need is the facts. You will be doing me a
great favor. If there is anything I can do for you
in return, let me know." Leslie had donned her
cloak of pseudo-sincerity.

"Oh, no; there is nothing." Elizabeth slowly
shook her head. "I— well, I wouldn't want you to
think I *cared* for a return." Her manner plainly
indicated that there was something Leslie might do
for her if she chose.

"What is it you want?" Leslie exhibited marked
impatience. "Favor for favor you know," she
added boldly. "I never mince matters."

"I am crazy to play on the soph basket-ball team.
Do you think you can fix it for me?"

"Surest thing ever. Leonard is peeved and has
tossed up sports. Two of the Sans are on committee. Is that all you need?"

"Yes." The wide babyish eyes registered a flash
of gratification. "You are *so kind,* Leslie. Thank
you a thousand times. I know you won't fail me."

"You're welcome. I'll fix it for you tomorrow.
One bit of advice. Don't play unless you are an
expert."

"I am. When I was at prep school——"

"Never mind about that now. You go ahead and tell me what I asked you. It is almost six and Nat will be here soon."

"Oh, will she?" The sophomore cast an apprehensive glance toward the door. "Is she a very good friend of Dulcie's?"

"She's a better friend of mine," was the bored reply. Leslie was growing tired of being kept from what she burned to know. "Please don't waste any more time, Bess. We can't talk after Nat comes in. I don't believe I'll be able to see you again before Saturday. I'm awfully busy. I'll lunch you at the Lotus then. We'll use my roadster for the trip to town. What?"

Elated at having gleaned from Leslie a promise of benefit to herself and an invitation to luncheon, Elizabeth once more stipulated that her name should be left out of the revelation. Again re-assured, she proceeded to regale Leslie with the confidences Dulcie had imparted to her at various times. She talked steadily for almost half an hour. Leslie gave her free rein, interrupting her but little.

"It's even worse than I had thought," Leslie declared grimly, when Elizabeth could recall nothing more to tell. "Bess, if you know when you are well off, you will never tell a soul what you have told me. Part of it isn't true. Dulcie was romancing to you about that hazing affair. We talked about it for fun, but that was all. Why, we were all at the masquerade that night."

"Dulcie wasn't," flatly contradicted the other. "She had a black eye. She said she was hurt at that house when——"

"Dulcie bumped into the door of her room that night with her mask on," interrupted Leslie angrily. "So she told us. If she was where she claims she was, certainly we were not with her. This isn't the first foolish rumor of the kind she has started. It's a good thing the rest of the girls don't know this. They'd never forgive Dulcie for starting such yarns. As for that trouble she claims we had with Miss Remson. There was nothing to that, either. We have never exchanged a word with Remson on the subject. I don't mind what she told you about the summons. The rest of her lies! Well, there is this much to it, Dulcie is due to hear from me and in short order."

CHAPTER XIV

SANS' MERCY

DESPITE Leslie's denials, Elizabeth left her room only half convinced. Being as lost to honor as Leslie, she was also as shrewd. She made a vow to keep her own counsel thereafter. She knew herself to be as guilty as Dulcie. She hoped Leslie would never discover that. Leslie had promised that her name should not be mentioned in the matter. If brought to book by Leslie, Dulcie could not accuse her of circulating the stories intrusted to her without incriminating herself. Elizabeth felt quite safe on that score.

For two or three days after her call upon Leslie, she kept out of Dulcie's way for fear the latter had been taken to task for her treachery and might suspect her as being instrumental in having brought it about. On Friday, however, she met Dulcie in the library. Dulcie invited her to dinner at the Colonial and she went without a tremor of conscience. The former was not in a gossiping humor that day. She was doing badly in all her subjects and worried in consequence.

Elizabeth went calmly to luncheon at the Lotus with Leslie on Saturday, pluming herself in chat she was on excellent terms with both factions. She reported to Leslie her meeting with Dulcie on Friday, saying lamely that Dulcie never gossiped a bit about the Sans. "She hadn't better," Leslie had returned vengefully. "She has done mischief enough already." When Elizabeth had ventured to inquire when Dulcie was to be "called down," Leslie had said, "When I get ready to do it. I'm not ready yet."

Natalie and Joan Myers had been informed by Leslie of Dulcie's treachery. The trio had then set to work to discover how much damage she had done; something not easy to determine. Natalie and Joan demanded that she should be dropped from the club. They were sure the others would be of the same mind. Even Eleanor Ray, her former chum, was on the outs with Dulcie. There would be no objection to the penalty from Eleanor. Leslie's plan was to gather the evidence against Dulcie, place it before the Sans, minus the culprit, at a private meeting, and let them decide her fate. In spite of Leslie Cairns' unscrupulous disposition, she had a queer sense of justice which occasionally stirred within her. Thus she was bent on being sure of her ground before accusing Dulcie to her face.

After a week had passed and the three had learned nothing new regarding the circulation of their misdeeds about the campus, Leslie called a meeting of the club in her room while Dulcie was absent from the Hall. Indignation ran high at the revelation. The verdict was, "Drop her from the club." Notwithstanding the possibility pointed out by Leslie that she might turn on them and betray them to headquarters, her associates were keen for dropping her.

"What harm can she do us?" argued Margaret Wayne. "She can't give us away to Doctor Matthews without cooking her own goose. That's our only danger from her. It's our word against hers. Any stories she has told on the campus will never go further than among the students. It is too bad! Dulcie should have known better than to be so utterly treacherous. She deserves to be dropped. We could never trust her again."

"That's what I think," concurred Joan Myers. "Even if her tales *did* bring about a private inquiry, it is our word against hers. We have really walked with a sword over our heads since last Saint Valentine's night. It has never fallen. I say, *simply fire* Dulcie from the Sans, and be done with it. Let it be a lesson to the rest of us to be discreet."

"When is the deed to be done?" Adelaide Forman inquired.

"I don't know yet. I want you girls to see what you can glean on the campus. I must have every scrap of evidence against her that I can get," Leslie announced. "We may not be able to spring it on her for a week or two. When we do, the meeting will be in this room. I'll hang a heavy curtain over the door so we won't be heard. If she gets very angry she will raise her voice to a positive shriek."

"Wouldn't it be better to hold that meeting outside the Hall? Dulcie will raise an awful fuss. If she hadn't told something I made her swear she wouldn't tell, I would not hear to having her treated that way. I am down on her for that very reason. Otherwise I would feel very sorry for her," explained Eleanor Ray.

"I am not on good terms with her. She made trouble between Evangeline and me last week. We only straightened it up today." Joan volunteered this information. "Leslie's room is the best place for the meeting. It is situated so that Dulcie won't be heard if she cries or flies into a temper."

While among the Sans there was not one girl who had not stooped to dishonorable acts since her entrance into Hamilton College, the fact of Dulcie's defection seemed monstrous indeed.

"Be careful what you say to Bess Walbert,"

Natalie took the liberty of saying. "How much does she know about what we shall do with Dulc? What did you tell her about it?"

"I said I had heard other things Dulcie had been saying; that she was due to hear from me for gossiping. That such yarns must be stopped. I warned her to keep to herself whatever Dulc had told her. She promised silence. I don't know." Leslie shrugged dubiously. "Take a leaf from Nat's book, girls, and keep mum to Bess. She may try to pump you. She's crazy to know what I am going to say to Dulc and when the fuss is to come off."

Natalie flushed her gratification of Leslie's approbation. The others received their leader's counsel with marked respect. The news of Dulcie's perfidy had given them food for uneasy reflection.

"We'll just have to depend on you, Les, to deal with Dulcie," Joan Myers said emphatically. "You can do it scientifically. Of course, we expect to stand by you. When the time comes you ought to do the talking."

"The firing, you mean," corrected Leslie, smiling in her most unpleasant fashion. "Leave it to me. It's our campus reputation against her feelings; if she has any. We all have a certain pride in ourselves as seniors. I'm not anxious to be looked down upon by the other classes. It is only a few months until Commencement. We must hang on until then, and at the same time keep up an appearance of senior dignity."

An assenting murmur arose. Allowed to do as they pleased by doting or careless parents, not one of the Sans would escape parental wrath were she to fail in her college course. Even more serious consequences would be attached to expellment.

"How are we to behave toward Dulcie?" was Eleanor Ray's question as the meeting broke up.

"As though nothing had happened," Leslie directed. "I shall take her by surprise. I wish her to be so completely broken up she won't have the nerve to fight back, either on the night of the fuss or afterward.

CHAPTER XV

PLANNING FOR OTHERS

WHILE the Sans were experiencing the discomfort of internal friction, the Lookouts and their friends were traveling the pleasant ways of harmony and peace. The sophomores had so thoroughly taken their freshman sisters under their genial wing that the juniors had little welfare work to do in that direction.

In the matter of basket ball they lost all active interest after the first game between the freshman and sophomore teams which took place on the first Saturday afternoon in November. The Sans still had friends enough among the seniors to make their influence felt in this respect. With two Sans elected to the sports committee, Professor Leonard had thrown up his hands in disgust after a vain attempt to get along pleasantly with the arrogant committee. He refused to be present at the try-out. Afterward he made it a point to be away from the gymnasium during team practice.

Leslie Cairns kept her word to Elizabeth Walbert to the letter. She was chosen by the committee to play on the official sophomore team. Phyllis Moore was also picked solely on account of her prowess. When she found herself on the same team with Elizabeth, she promptly resigned.

The freshman team was picked by the committee entirely according to Sans tactics. Therefore, the democratic element of Hamilton foresaw a series of uninteresting games ahead. Dutifully they attended the initial game of the season which the sophs won. Most of the applause came from the seniors present at the game. According to Muriel Harding, she had seen better games played by the grammar school children of Sanford.

Basket ball thus failing to arouse their marked

enthusiasm, the former faithful fans and expert
players turned their moments of recreation into
channels which pleased them better. Incidental with
the decline of basket ball, Marjorie and Robin took
to looking earnestly about them for a motive for
the entertainments they had discussed giving.

Marjorie scouted about diligently in an effort to
locate students off the campus who needed financial
help. She took Anna Towne into her confidence at
last and found out something of interest.

"It isn't half so much that most of the girls living off the campus can't pull themselves through
college. They manage to do it by working through
the summer vacations. It is the way we have to
live that is so nerve-racking at times. The food
isn't always good, and there's so little variety if one
boards. The girls who cook for themselves have
to market. That's a strain. One is out of bread
or butter or another staple and forgets all about it
until supper time. Then the small stores nearby are
closed. Perhaps one wishes to spend an hour or
two in the library after recitations. There is the
marketing to do, or else it has to be done early in
the morning when one is hurrying to get ready for
a first recitation. That's merely one of the difficul-
ties attached to trying to lead the student life and
doing light house-keeping at the same time.

"On the other hand," Anna had further explained,

"if one boards one isn't always allowed to do one's own laundering. That's quite an item of expense. It costs more in money to board, and it is more of an expense of spirit to keep house on a small scale. It is a great irritation either way. That is the opinion of every girl off the campus I have talked with. You girls in your beautiful campus house are lucky. Many of these boarding and rooming houses are so cold in winter. For the amount of board or rental we pay the proprietors claim they can't afford to give adequate heat.

"You see, Marjorie, when girls like myself decide on enrolling at a certain college, they have only the prospectus to go by. They read in the Bulletin of Students' Aids and Bureaus of Self-help but they do not reckon on them. They go to college on their own resources. They wouldn't dream of asking help as freshmen; perhaps not at all during their whole course."

"I see," Marjorie had assented very soberly. It hurt her to hear of the struggles for an education going on so near her, while she had everything and more than heart could desire. "There ought to be one or two houses on the campus where students could live as cheaply as in boarding and rooming houses and still have their time entirely for study and recreation."

"That won't be in my time at Hamilton," Anna

had declared with a tired little smile. "I hope it will happen some day."

When Marjorie had left Anna, it was with a certain generous resolve. That night she made it known to Jerry.

"Do you know what I am going to do?" she asked, after recounting to her room-mate her conversation of the afternoon.

"I do not. I'll be pleased to hear your remarks, whatever they may be," encouraged Jerry with one of her wide smiles.

"You know what a lot of vacancies there will be here in June," Marjorie began. "Those vacancies ought to be filled by off-the-campus girls. Take Anna, for instance. She earns about one-third enough money summers to keep her at Wayland Hall. I shall furnish the other two-thirds for her. I shall begin now and save something from my allowance toward it. I shall ask Captain not to buy me a lot of new clothes for next year, but to give me the money instead. I am going to do a little sacrificing. I shall cut out dinners and luncheons off the campus. I'll go only to Baretti's and not so very often."

"We are an extravagant set," Jerry confessed. "Our board is paid at the Hall; the very best board, too. Yet away we go every two or three days for a feed at our favorite tea-rooms. That's a good idea,

Marvelous Manager. I shall presently adopt an off-the-campusite myself. Ronny will adopt a dozen."

"Ronny would finance them all, but I sha'n't let her. General would give me the money to see Anna through college, but I don't wish it to be that way. I want it to be self-denial money. I'd like to find a way to help the off-the-campus girls *this* year."

"Give shows. Make money. Turn it over to 'em," suggested Jerry, with an airy wave of the hand. "Nothing easier."

"Nothing harder, you mean," corrected Marjorie. "They wouldn't like to accept it as a private gift, I'm afraid. Besides, some of them board; others do light housekeeping. Those who keep house could use the money we offered to make things easier. Still they'd have the strain of housework on their minds. Those who board wouldn't be benefited much unless they changed boarding places. There is only that one collection of boarding houses near the campus. One is about the same as another. Hamilton has been a rich girls' college for a long time. The fine equipment and super-excellent faculty have filled it up with well-to-do and moneyed students."

"I'd like to see every Hamilton student on the campus," declared Jerry heartily. "It would take three campus houses to do it. There must be close to seventy-five girls in that bunch of off-campus houses."

"We could start our fund for that purpose," was the hopeful response.

"Who'd take care of the plan after we were graduated? It would take a lot of money to build campus houses. Besides, how would we get the site? Maybe the Board wouldn't hear to the project."

"Too true, too true, Jeremiah," Marjorie conceded gayly. "That plan is a little far-fetched just yet. Later it may seem feasible. The fact remains that Robin and I yearn to get up a show; object to give away the proceeds."

"You can do this. Arrange for the show. Advertise it as being given for the purpose of founding a students' beneficiary association. Take a third of the proceeds and start the society. Give the other two-thirds to Anna and let her distribute it privately among the girls who need it. She knows them. She can get away with it better than you can. If anyone comes down on the treasury for our little lone third we can hand it out and keep it up by private contributions until some more money is earned. I suppose you two marvelous managers will continue in the show business as long as it is profitable."

"Your head is level, Jeremiah," laughed Marjorie, her eyes sparkling. "That's a good plan. I'll see Robin tomorrow, and Anna too. Robin can begin to gather up the performers. Anna can find out for me as to how her flock are situated. I shall call the girls in tomorrow evening and ask them if they each would like to finance a student next year. Leila, Vera and Helen will like to, even if they have been graduated from Hamilton. Kathie can't, but she will wish to help in some other way."

"Anna Towne was my freshie catch. You may have her. I'll scout around and find someone else," magnanimously accorded Jerry.

Marjorie spent her leisure hours during the ensuing few days in interviewing her friends and helping Robin plan the show. With Thanksgiving only ten days off, the show would not take place until after that holiday. The girls tackled the programme, however, and completed it within three days.

Ronny was to dance twice. Marjorie had written to Constance Stevens, who had promised to sing at the revue. These two numbers were to be the features. The Silverton Hall orchestra would contribute two numbers. Leila and Vera had promised an ancient Irish contra dance in castume. Phyllis would give a violin solo. Blanche Scott would offer a grand opera selection in her best baritone voice. Ronny agreed to train eight girls in a singing and dancing number. As a wind-up, four Acasia House girls were to put on a one-act French play.

Busy with her new project, Marjorie had not forgotten Miss Susanna. The day after her visit to Hamilton Arms she had written the old lady one of her sincere, friendly notes. She had not expected a reply. Nevertheless, Miss Hamilton had returned a few lines of acknowledgment. Since then the wires of communication betwen them had been idle.

Marjorie regretted this. She would have liked, during the beautiful autumn weather, to walk about the grounds of Hamilton Arms with its owner. With the last leaves off the trees and the earth frost-bitten, she began to feel that Miss Susanna had not desired her further acquaintance. In passing Hamilton Arms she strained her eyes, invariably, for a sight of the old lady. She saw her but once, and at a distance.

She wondered as Thanksgiving approached what kind of Thanksgiving Miss Hamilton would have. She resolved, before leaving college for home, to write the last of the Hamiltons as cheerful a note as she could compose.

Three days before college closed for the holiday she found a letter in the Hall bulletin board in Miss

Susanna's handwriting. This letter bore the ad-dress "Wayland Hall," and read:

"DEAR CHILD:

"I have a curiosity to meet some of the young women you exalted to me when you took tea at the Arms. Will you bring them with you to five o'clock tea tomorrow afternoon? I had intended writing you before this date, but have been ill and out of sorts. I believe you mentioned eight young women as your particular friends. I can entertain you and the beloved eight, but no more. Do not trouble to answer this note. I shall expect to se you, even if the others can't come to tea.

"Yours sincerely,
                    "SUSANNA CRAIG HAMILTON."

Marjorie uttered a kind of exultant crow and performed a funny little dance of jubilation about the room. Jerry had not yet come from recitations, so she hurried out to find the other Lookouts. Ronny was the only one in. She rejoiced with Marjorie, her interest in Hamilton Arms and its owner being second only to that of her chum.

"She loves flowers. We must take her a big box of roses," was Marjorie's generous thought. "Pink, white and red ones; yellow roses, too, if we can find them. It is hard to find a certain kind of fragrant, very double yellow rose at the florist's now."

"You mean 'Perle de Jaddin,'" Ronny said quickly. "We have acres of them at 'Manana.' They are my favorite rose."

"I love them, too," Marjorie nodded. "I remember that name now. I will collect two dollars apiece from the girls. Two times nine are eighteen. We ought to be able to buy an armful of roses for eighteen dollars. I'll ask Leila to drive to Hamilton for them. She has no class the last hour. I think we had better walk to Hamilton Arms. Miss Susanna seems to be rather down on girls who drive cars. So there is no use in flaunting her dislike in her face. I may be in error on that point. She made a remark on the day I met her that led me to think so."

"You go and find the other girls. I'll tell Lucy as soon as she comes in," Ronny offered. "The sooner you see them, the better. If they have engagements for tomorrow afternoon they will have to gracefully slide out of them. We all must accept Miss Susanna's invitation. It is a case of now or never."

Marjorie left Ronny to go joyfully on her pleasant errand. Her second quest was more successful. Leila and Vera had returned while she was in Ronny's room. Both were elated over the unexpected honor. Leila was more than willing to make the trip to the florist's shop.   Marjorie met Katherine in the hall just as she was leaving Leila's room.

The trio of absentees, Helen, Muriel and Jerry, she decided must be out somewhere together. She smiled to herself as she pictured Jerry's face when she heard the news. "Just because I am in a hurry to tell Jerry she will probably go to dinner off the campus and come marching in about nine o'clock," was her half-vexed rumination.

To her satisfaction Jerry walked into the room at ten minutes to six. She and Helen had taken a ride in the latter's car. Jerry was full of mirth over the fact that they had met Elizabeth Walbert's car at the side of the road with a blown-out tire. A mechanician from a Hamilton garage was on the scene adjusting a new one under the verbose direction of the owner.

"Helen drove her car past at a crawl. We wanted to hear what she was saying to the man from the garage. Honestly, we could hear her voice before we came very near her. She shrieks at the top of her lungs. She was trying to tell him what to do. He wasn't paying any more attention to her than if she hadn't been there. That blond freshie, who snubbed Phil the day she tried to help her at the station, was with her. I heard her say, 'My, but he is slow. Our chauffeur could have put on three tires while he was thinking about putting on one.' So encouraging to the workman!" Jerry's tones registered gleeful sarcasm. "I wish she had been stuck there for about four hours."

"You should not rejoice at the downfall of others," Marjorie reproved with a giggle. "That is, if you can class a bursted tire as a downfall."

"It did me a world of good to see those two little snips stuck at the side of the road," returned Jerry. "That Walbert girl and her car are a joke. I wish we had a college paper. I'd write her up. Funny there isn't one at Hamilton. Almost every other college has one, sometimes two. I think I shall start one next year, if I'm not too busy."

"You might call it 'Jeremiah's Journal,'" suggested Marjorie. Both girls laughed at this conceit. Marjorie then acquainted her room-mate with the invitation, at the same time handing her Miss Hamilton's note.

"Will wonders never cease!" Jerry laid down the note and beamed at Marjorie. "All your fault, Marvelous Manager. You went ahead and paved the way into Miss Susanna's good graces for the rest of us. You certainly do get on the soft side of people without trying."

"Not a bit of it," Marjorie stoutly contested. "Any one of you girls would have done as I did and with the same results. I am so glad you are all going to meet her. She can't help but have a better opinion of our dear old Alma Mater after she has met some of her nicest children. I guess that basket handle broke at the psychological moment."

CHAPTER XVI

OUT OF THE PAST

THE invited guests were in scarcely more of an anticipatory flutter than Miss Susanna herself. She had broken down her prejudice against girls partly out of curiosity to see and know Marjorie's friends, partly because of her growing fondness for Marjorie. The innocent beauty of the young girl, and her utter lack of conceit and affectation, had made a deep impression on the suspicious, embittered old lady. She had no expectation of liking Marjorie's friends as she was learning to like the courteous, gracious lieutenant. It was her skeptical opinion, uttered to Jonas, that, if *one* of the "new ones" turned out to be half as worthy as "that pretty child," she would not regret the experiment.

"You may take me for an old fool, Jonas," she declared to her faithful servitor of many years. "Here I am entertaining college misses after I've sworn enmity against them for so long. Well, everything once, Jonas; everything once. If I don't like 'em, they won't be invited here again."

"The young lady's friends will be all right, Miss Susanna," Jonas had earnestly assured. "She is fine little lady."

The "young lady's friends," however, were seized with a certain amount of trepidation when, on the designated afternoon, they advanced on Hamilton Arms, looking their prettiest. Each had worn the afternoon frock she liked best in honor of her hostess. Marjorie, Leila and Jerry headed the van, Leila bearing in her arms a huge box of roses. Marjorie had insisted that Leila must present these to Miss Susanna. Leila had sturdily demurred, then accepted the honor thrust upon her. All the way to Hamilton Arms she had kept the party in a gale of laughter with the humorous presentation speeches which she framed en route.

Within a few steps of the house her fund of words deserted her. "Take these yourself, Marjorie," she implored. "I am in too much of a glee at my own foolishness. I shall laugh and disgrace us all if I undertake to give her the roses."

"You'll be all right, you goose. I refuse to help you out." Marjorie waved aside the proffered box. "Rally your nerve and say the first thing that occurs to you. It will be sure to be the best thing you could possibly say."

"I doubt it. Well, I can but take firm hold on the box and make the best of a bad matter." Leila grasped the box with exaggerated force, cleared her throat and burst out laughing. She continued to laugh as they ascended the steps. She had hardly straightened her face when Jonas answered the door and ushered the guests over the threshold they had never expected to cross.

"I have not seen so many girls at close range for a long time," announced a brisk voice. Miss Susanna had come from the library into the hall to greet her visitors. She was attired in a one-piece dress of dark gray silk with a white fichu at the throat of frost-like lace.

"How are you, my child?" She now took Marjorie's hand. "And these are your friends." Her bright brown eyes were inspecting the group of young women with a kind of reflective curiosity. "Introduce them to me and tell me each name slowly. I wish to know each one by name from now on. I used to have a good memory for names."

Marjorie complied with the instruction, adding some friendly little point descriptive of each chum. This evoked laughter and helped to ease the slight strain attached to the presentation. Leila then proffered the box of roses with a frank, "Here is our good will to you, Miss Hamilton."

"What's this?" Miss Susanna viewed the long box in amazement. A swift tide of color rose to her cheeks. She reached for it mechanically as though uncertain what to do next. She held it for an instant, then said: "I thank you, girls. You could have done nothing that would please me more. I love flowers; particularly roses. Come into the library now and let us get acquainted."

In the library Miss Susanna explored the florist's box with the pleasure of a child. She exclaimed happily over the masses of gorgeous roses as she lifted them from the box and inhaled their fragrance. She sent Jonas for vases and arranged them to suit her fancy, talking animatedly to her guests as her small hands busied themselves with the pleasant task.

The girls gathered informally about her, looking on with gratified eyes. The flower gift had established a bond of sympathy between them. Already Miss Susanna was beginning to glimpse the reason for Marjorie's devotion to her special friends. The girls also understood Marjorie's growing interest in the last of the Hamiltons. Miss Hamilton had an oddly fascinating personality which commanded liking.

"There!" Miss Susanna exclaimed, as the last

rose went into a vase to her satisfaction. "I shall
leave them in the library while you are here. Afterward I shall take my posies to my room. They will
be the last thing I see tonight and the first in the
morning. I have selfishly fussed with my lovely
roses instead of giving you hungry children your
tea. We are going to have it in the tea room today.
I will ask you to come now."

She led the way from the library to an apartment
directly behind it. A subdued chorus of admiration
ascended from the guests as they stepped into a
room which was quite Chinese in character. The
walls were hung with rare Chinese embroideries
and delicately-tinted prints. A pale green matting
rug with intricately-wrought lavender and buff
characters covered the floor. The tables and chairs
were of polished teak, beautifully inlaid with mother
of pearl. In one corner was a tall Chinese cabinet
topped by two exquisite peachblow vases. Here and
there were other vases of value and beauty. It was
an amazing room. With so much to look at, it
required time to appreciate fully its worth from an
artistic point of view.

While there were several small tables, there was
a large oblong one which would seat the party. It
was laid for tea and graced by the most wonderful
tea set the girls had ever seen. It was of faint,

almost translucent, green banded by an odd Chinese scroll border in silver.

"What a perfectly wonderful room!" gasped Vera, her hands coming together in an admiring clasp, so characteristic of her.

Her approval was echoed by the others. The mistress of Hamilton Arms piloted them to the large table, taking her place at the head of it.

"Have your tea first, then you may explore Uncle Brooke's famous tea room as much as you please." Miss Susanna glanced about at the circle of eager young faces with a bright smile. She was enjoying this innovation so much more than she had thought she might. "This will really be a meat tea. I know you girls will need something more substantial than tea and cakes, as you won't be home in time for dinner."

The invaluable Jonas now appearing, an appetizing collation consisting of creamed chicken, hot muffins, a salad and sweets was served, together with much tea and more talk and laughter. The girls were hungry enough to enjoy every mouthful of the delicious food provided by their hostess, agreeing with Marjorie as to the super-excellence of the tea.

"Please tell us about this tea room, Miss Susanna," coaxed Marjorie. The repast finished, the party still sat at table. "I suppose it was planned and arranged by Mr. Brooke Hamilton."

"Yes; it is considered the finest private tea room in America," was the reply. The odd part of this room is that every article in it was a gift to my great uncle. Shortly after LaFayette's visit to America, when Uncle Brooke was a young man in his early twenties, he embarked on a business venture to China. He expected to be gone only a year. Instead, he remained in China for twelve years. Unlike many persons, he did not antagonize the Chinese. They learned to appreciate him for his nobility, and became his firm friends. Every now and then, someone would make him a present. A true Chinaman will give the best he has if he wishes to give.

"Uncle Brooke was so much pleased with his growing collection of things Chinese, that he announced his intention of having a Chinese room in his home when he returned to America," continued the old lady, a gleam of pride in her eyes. "He told his Chinese friends of his idea and they were delighted. Eventually a rich noble, who had been one of Uncle Brooke's truest friends, died. He bequeathed a priceless collection of Chinese antiquities to my ancestor. Among them was this tea set, those two peachblow vases, and that print on the east wall. When he returned to America it took him six months to arrange this room to his satisfaction. He arranged it and pulled it to pieces dozens of times before he produced the effect he desired."

"Do you remember him, Miss Susanna?" asked Marjorie eagerly, then blushed for fear her question might be considered too pointed by her hostess.

"Very well, indeed. I was a young woman when he died. He was seventy-nine years old the week before his death. My father was the son of his only brother who was several years older than Uncle Brooke. Father was an invalid during the last years of his life. We came here to live when I was twelve. As a child, Uncle Brooke would often take me for walks about the estate. He taught me the names and habits of trees, shrubs and flowers. He was a true nature man."

"It seems odd to hear so much, all at once, of Mr. Brooke Hamilton," observed Helen. "We have not heard anything of him before except what little is known on the campus. He is almost a mystery at Hamilton College."

"The fault of the college," retorted Miss Susanna with bitterness. "There was a time when the college board might have had the data for his biography. That time has passed. They shall never have one scrap of information concerning him from me. What I have told you of him today is in strict confidence. I have spoken freely of him because Mar-

jorie has assured me that you are to be trusted.
Were you to break this confidence, I would refuse
to verify whatever you might tell and forbid any
publication of the information."

Miss Hamilton glanced defiantly about the circle.
Her kindly expression had entirely vanished.

"We can but assure you of our discretion." It
was Leila who made an answer, a hint of wounded
pride in her blue eyes.

"You can trust us, Miss Susanna," added Marjorie, smiling bravely. She was experiencing a
queer little sinking of the heart at the displeased old
lady's intent to permanently withhold from the college the true history of its founder.

"I daresay I can, child. Let us change the subject. It is unpleasant to me. You girls had better
walk about the tea room and enjoy the curios until
I recover my good humor."

Prompt to obey the mandate, the girls spent at
least a half hour in the Oriental room, examining
and admiring the departed connoisseur's individual
arrangement of a marvelous collection. Miss Susanna sat and watched them, almost moodily. Returned to the library, the sight of her roses mollified
her. She decided to do a certain thing which had
risen to her mind. The desire to give pleasure to
these young girls who had thought of her conquered
her sudden gust of spleen against Hamilton College.

"Would you like to see my great uncle's study?" she asked, turning from the flowers to her guests.

"Oh!" Ronny drew a wondering audible breath. She could hardly believe her ears.

The others laughed at her, but the eager light in their eyes told its own story.

"May we see it, Miss Susanna?" Vera's tone was almost imploring.

"You may. Another time, when all of you come to see me, I will show you about the house. It is well worth seeing. My great uncle gathered beauty from the four corners of the earth. He loved to travel and brought back with him the treasure of other lands. I should like you to see the study. It holds one thing, in particular, in which I am sure you will be interested."

"There is no corner of this house without interest," Leila said warmly. "I am sure of that."

"So it seems to me," nodded Miss Hamilton. "I have lived in it many years. I am not over the wonder of it yet. At times I am sorry that others cannot enjoy it with me. Again I am glad to be alone."

Following the old lady, who mounted the broad staircase as nimbly as any of them, they found on the second landing the same solid magnificence of furnishing that marked the first floor. Down a long hallway, which extended back from the main reception hall, they went. At the end of the hall was a door of heavy walnut, its upper half of stained glass. This their guide opened. They were now seeing the room where the founder of Hamilton College had spent so many hours planning the institution which bore his name.

The murmur of voices died out among them as they stepped into the study. Compared with other rooms in the house which the girls had seen, it was rather small. The floor was bare save for one medium-sized rug in the center of the room, on which stood a heavy-legged mahogany writing table. A tall desk, a book-case, three high-backed chairs and a filing cabinet, all of carved mahogany, completed the furnishings, plus one broad-seated chair, leather cushioned, and with a rounding back. It was drawn up before the library table; Brooke Hamilton's own chair.

The most notable object in the study was a framed, illuminated oblong about five feet long and perhaps two and a half feet wide. It was hung at a point on the wall directly opposite the founder's chair.

"This is what you wished us to see, isn't it?" Marjorie cried out, stopping in front of the oblong. "I think I know what it is."

"Tell us, then." Miss Susanna was smiling fondly at the animated face Marjorie turned toward her.

"The maxims of Mr. Brooke Hamilton," she guessed breathlessly. Her eyes traveled slowly down the oblong. "There are fifteen of them," she announced. "What a beautiful illumination!"

"Yes; they were his favorite sayings. He originated them all except the first one. More, he lived up to them." The old lady's intonation had grown singularly gentle.

A reverent silence visited the study as the knot of girls gathered about the oblong to read the sayings of one long gone from earth. The colors used in the illumination were principally blue and gold with mere touches of green and black. Red had been left out entirely from the color scheme.

"Remember the stranger within thy gates."

"To the wise nothing is forbidden."

"Becoming earnestness is never out of place."

"Let thy gratitude be lasting."

"Ask Heaven for courtesy; the supply is greater than the demand."

"Make thy deference to age not too marked."

"Truth flies a winning pennant."

"Beware, lest what seems unattainable falls too near thine hand."

"Let thy learning be seasoned with merriment."

"O, Justice, how fair art thine heights!"

"Be motivated by the grace of God."

"Be not secret; be discreet."

"For the gift of life give thanks."

"The ways of light reach upward to eternity."

"To stumble honorably is to learn to walk."

Such were the informal rules of conduct which Brooke Hamilton had carved for himself with the blade of experience.

"We have five of these at the college, Miss Susanna." Ronny finally broke the spell which had fallen. "The first, third, fourth, seventh and ninth. 'Remember the stranger within thy gates,' is over the doorway of Hamilton Hall. The ninth one is in the library and the third, fourth and seventh are in the chapel."

"I knew some of them were there. The first he had placed over the door of Hamilton Hall. The others were to be presented to the college as the students earned them."

"Earned them?" queried Muriel impulsively. "I don't understand——" She broke off, coloring at her own temerity. Her companions were also looking slightly mystified.

"His idea was this. He wished to reward any particularly noteworthy act on the part of a student, of which he chanced to hear, by an honor. The recipient was to receive a citation in chapel and one of his favorite maxims, decoratively framed, was to be hung in one of the campus buildings. A record of the citation was to be established in an honor book kept in a special niche in the chapel. This was one of his later ideas. He did not live to carry it out. I don't know how they managed to get hold of four of his sayings. They have no right to them."

Acridity again dominated Miss Susanna's tones. She appeared to resent deeply the fact that the college authorities held any information whatsoever regarding her famous kinsman.

"Maybe a person who knew your great uncle remembered these four maxims of his and they were thus handed down," suggested Lucy, always interested in a mystery.

"I wish we had them all; everyone of them!" Marjorie gave an audible sigh of regret. "I can't help saying it, Miss Susanna. It is the way I feel about these true, wonderful sayings of Mr. Brooke Hamilton."

"You may say it without offending me, my dear. I understand you and your affection for Hamilton College. *He* would have liked you to say it. *He* never held a grudge. I have held one many years. I shall continue to hold it." Miss Susanna crested her stubborn head. "It is a supreme pleasure to me to know that I have thwarted the college board in some respects. I shall continue to thwart them."

CHAPTER XVII

LUCY'S NEWS

ON the heels of their memorable visit to Hamilton Arms came the added joy of going home for Thanksgiving. All the pleasure that the occasion afforded was crowded into those four brief days. The Nine Travelers, as they agreed to call themselves, returned to college more firmly amalgamated than ever.

The Lookouts had long since included their four close friends in the formal association which they had dubbed the Five Travelers. At first they had decided that the name should remain the same, though four members were added. Later, Ronny suggested that Nine Travelers would be more appropriate. At the end of their college course, they would choose nine girls to replace them with a new chapter, as they had done in the case of the Lookout Club. All nine were anxious to leave a sorority behind them of which they could claim to have founded.

Marjorie and Robin Page, who, according to

Jerry, "had gone into the show business," had their hands full the moment they returned to Hamilton. They tackled the enterprise with a will, however, and within a couple of days after resuming the difficult duties of managership they had made considerable headway.

"Have you those posters yet?" greeted Robin, as she joyfully pounced upon Marjorie on the steps of the library. "I have been trying to see you ever since yesterday morning. I was coming over last night, but I simply had to stay at home and study. I struck a horrible snag in calculus and struggled with it half the evening."

"Ethel said she would have them done tomorrow," was the comforting news. "She made four. I imagine they must be beauties, too."

"Uh-h-h!" Robin pretended to crumple with relief. "That's one torture off my mind. Naturally they will be great stuff. Ethel Laird draws better than any other girl at Hamilton. It was mighty fine in her to take such a job on herself. I asked her for only one you know."

"Probably she saw a wistful gleam in your eye and was kind," laughed Marjorie.

"There will be an entirely different gleam in my eye if those printers don't hurry up with the programmes. Last I heard from them they hadn't even started the work. We really took a good deal upon ourselves when we started this show. I'm glad I am not a manager for my living. It is too strenuous a life for Robin."

"We ought to call a rehearsal Saturday evening. There won't be anyone caring to use the gym, and there won't be much time for it next week in the evenings. with all the studying we have to do. Just recall, the show is to be next Friday evening," was Marjorie's reminder.

"Oh, I know it," groaned Robin. "I shall be enraged, infuriated and foaming at the mouth if those aggravating printers don't have our programmes done in time."

"They will. Don't worry. When did they promise you the tickets?"

"Tomorrow. They've done fairly well with the tickets," Robin grudgingly conceded. "That is, provided they deliver them tomorrow, as promised. I am just a little tired, I guess. I like the programme part of getting up a show, but I don't like the tiresome details."

"Come on over to Baretti's," invited Marjorie. "What you need is sustenance. We can talk things over and have dinner at the same time. I can stay out until eight. It's only five-fifteen now. We shall have oceans of time."

"All right. Don't you believe, though, that we'll

have much chance to talk. Some of our gang will be there, sure as fate," Robin prognosticated.

Surely enough, they were greeted by a hospitable quartette occupying a table near the door. It was composed of Ronny, Jerry, Elaine Hunter and Barbara Severn.

"Aren't you going home to dinner?" quizzed Jerry accusingly. "And you never said a word to me this noon of your secret intentions."

"I hadn't any. May I ask why you are here without having obtained my permission?" Marjorie drew down her face in an imitation of Miss Merton, a Sanford teacher both girls had greatly disliked.

"I have nothing to say," chuckled Jerry. "You and your friend may sit at our table, if you like."

"Thank you. My friend and I have weighty matters to discuss. We're in the show business now, Jeremiah. We are bound for that last table in the row." Marjorie pointed. "We'll join you later, and please don't disturb us. Ahem!"

"I don't even know either of you by sight. Beat it." Jerry waved both girls away with a magnificent gesture of disdain which sent them giggling toward their table.

"This is my first off-the-campus treat since we talked about getting up the show that day we went to Hamilton," Marjorie confided to Robin. I have thirty-eight dollars saved. Captain gave me twenty-

five when I came away from home. I told her I
did not need it, but you see I had told her about
saving my money, too. That's the reason she gave
it to me. I seem not to be able to make any real
sacrifices," Marjorie smiled ruefully.

"I have saved close to thirty. I could have saved
more, but I have had three Silvertonites to remember on their birthdays. Not my pals, but girls who
appreciate remembrances and who don't receive
many. I haven't been here but twice since we had
that talk. We mustn't desert Signor Baretti, either.
He would feel dreadfully if we stopped patronizing
his tea room."

"We will have to try to please all our friends
somehow, and ourselves, too," Marjorie said gayly.

Their dinner ordered, the two settled down to
talk over the progress of their "show" with the
business energy of two real theatrical managers.
Later, however, Jerry and her trio sidled up to the
forbidden table and were graciously allowed to
remain. In consequence, it was half-past eight
before the party left the tea room.

"Lucy will wonder what has become of me,"
Ronny declared, as the three Lookouts entered
Wayland Hall. "I told her this noon I was not going
anywhere after recitations. Oh, dear! I am a
nice person! I promised to help Muriel with her

French, before dinner. I forgot all about it until this minute. She will be raving."

"You seem to be in a bad case all around," sympathized Jerry in most unsympathetic tones. "I'm sorry for you."

"I'm a great deal more sorry for myself," retorted Jerry.

"I haven't broken any promise by staying out, but I won't do much studying tonight. Let me see, what recitations do I have tomorrow that I can slight the least tiny bit?" Marjorie puckered her brows over her problem.

Entering their room, the first sight that me hers and Jerry's eyes was Lucy Warner, fast asleep in an arm chair. Jerry laid a warning finger against her lips, then she stole softly up to Lucy.

"Wake up and pay for your lodgings," she growled in a deep, hoarse voice.

"Oh-h! Ah-h!" Lucy sat up with a suddenness which narrowly missed landing her on the floor. "I thought you would never come home," she mumbled, not yet fully awake. Blinking sleepily at the two laughing girls, she continued: "I had some news for you. I sat down to wait until you came. Ronny was out; so was Muriel. I've been here since eight o'clock. Were you out to dinner?"

"That means *you* were not here." Jerry pointed an arraigning finger at Lucy. "Where have you been?   Lately you have become a regular gad-about.   It must be stopped, Luciferous."

"Gad-about nothing," disclaimed Lucy.   "You, not I, belong to that deplorable class, Jeremiah Macy.   *I* have been working.   True, I dined out-side the Hall, and in distinguished company.   I am President Matthews' secretary pro tem.   I had din-ner at his house tonight.   I told you I had news for you."

"Can you beat that?"   Jerry sank into the near-est chair as though about to collapse.   "You are mounting the college scale by leaps and bounds, aren't you?   Chummy with the registrar, a friend of Professor Wenderblatt's, and now established in Doctor Matthews' good graces.   The unprece-dented rise of Luciferous Warniferous; or, Secreta-ries who have become famous."

"How did it happen?   Where is Miss Sayres?" Marjorie exhibited lively curiosity at the news.

"Miss Sayres is at home with a cold.   Nothing very serious, I imagine.   Miss Humphrey recom-mended me to the doctor.   He was away behind in his correspondence.   Miss Sayres has been ill for two days.   It was nearly six when I finished his letters.   He still had an address to dictate.   He asked me if I would stay until after dinner and take the dictation.   I had a beautiful time.   He and his wife are such friendly persons.   He is a great biologist, too. His son was there. He is a New York lawyer and is home for a few days' visit." Lucy added this last without enthusiasm.

"Well, well, Luciferous!" patronized Jerry. "And were you afraid to talk to the young man?"

"Oh, stop teasing me! No, I was not. He talked to his mother most of the time, anyway. I must go and find Ronny. Was she with you girls?" Lucy rose, gathered her books from the table, and prepared to depart.

"She was with us, Lucy. You'd better stay and talk to us," coaxed Marjorie. "It's growing later and later and still I am not studying. I might as well wind up a pleasant but unprofitable evening with gossiping about Doctor Matthews. Come on back and resume your chair, Miss Warner."

Lucy had now reached the door. "Wait until I go and see Ronny, and I will come back." She exited, returning five minutes afterward with Ronny.

"You don't seem to have the study habit tonight, either," commented Jerry genially to the new arrival. Well, sit down and have a good time. That's what college is for."

"How do you like the doctor, Lucy?" There was a note of sharp interest in the question. Marjorie was anxious to hear Lucy's opinion of the presi-

'dent. "I know you said he was friendly; but, I mean, what do you think of him in other ways?"

"I understand you. You are thinking of Miss Remson. So was I, whenever I had a chance to study the man. He is one of the kindest, finest men I have ever come in contact with," Lucy declared impressively. "He is so courteous; he goes to great pains in answering his letters. I know he never wrote that letter to Miss Remson."

"I felt that way about him, too, the day I played messenger for Miss Humphrey." Marjorie nodded agreement of Lucy's emphatic praise.

"I wish I could solve that letter mystery while I am there." Lucy's green eyes gleamed. "My one chance would be to have a talk about it with Doctor Matthews. That's not likely to happen. I could find out a good deal about Miss Sayres by going through the letter files, but I would die rather than touch one of them. I shall only be there for a day or two, I suppose. If I could be his secretary for two or three weeks I might be able to say a good word for Miss Remson. I am sure there has been a great misrepresentation and I believe Miss Sayres is at the bottom of it."

"What would you do, Luciferous, if, while you were there, you found out something that was plain proof against the Sans?" was Marjorie's thoughtful query.

"I would take it up with Doctor Matthews at once, wouldn't you, in the same circumstances?"

"Yes," came the unhesitating reply. "That is the one thing I have always thought I would not mind telling against the Sans." Marjorie's features grew sternly determined. "It was such a cruel thing to do; to estrange two friends of such long standing. For all we know, Doctor Matthews may wonder why Miss Remson has not visited him and his wife for over a year."

"It is not likely that I shall find any such proof. If I should, I would use it very quickly. Miss Remson was dreadfully hurt over that miserable letter. I would put the proof before Doctor Matthews if I had to fight all the Sans single-handed afterward."

CHAPTER XVIII

WHEN FRIENDS BECOME FOES

LUCY's secretaryship for Doctor Matthews lasted only three days. During that short space of time she found out nothing special, bearing on the wrong to Miss Remson which she longed to right. She learned to like the president of Hamilton College better than ever, and wished she might work for him longer. The only item of interest she came across was at his residence. In the secretary's desk there she discovered the New York address of Leslie Cairns in a small red leather address book. To her analytical mind this was proof enough of an acquaintance between the two.

She had not expected to do anything of moment toward helping Miss Remson during those three days. Still she could not help confessing to Marjorie that she was a wee bit disappointed at not having learned a single thing.

"Never mind, Luciferous," Marjorie had consoled. "You had the will to help Miss Remson if you did not have the opportunity. It may all come to light when you least expect it. That's the way such things often happen."

While Lucy had deplored her inability to obtain the desired information she legitimately sought, the Sans loudly deplored among themselves her temporary appointment as secretary. Coupled with it a story had reached the ears of Natalie Weyman and Joan Myers which caused them to flee to Leslie Cairns in a hurry. It had to do with the hazing party the previous February. Joan had been slyly taxed with it first. Pretending innocence, she had made an excuse to leave the senior who had intimated it to her without having betrayed herself in any particular.

Several days afterward she and Natalie Weyman had gone through almost the same experience with two juniors who had appeared to treat the affair as a huge joke. The girl who had first hinted it to Joan had been rather horrified over what she had evidently heard.

"I think it is high time we called Dulcie Vale to account!" Natalie exclaimed stormily, as she finished the recital of what she and Joan had just heard.

The two had burst in upon Leslie, regardless of the "Busy" sign which now ornamented her door a good deal of the time when she was in her room.

"Calm down, Nat. You are so mad you are fairly shouting. Take seats and have some candy, both of you." Leslie lazily pushed a huge box of nut chocolates across the table within easy reach of her excited callers.

"Um-m! Glaucaire's best!" Natalie forgot her wrath and helped herself to sweets.

"I had made up my mind before you two burst in with your tale of woe that Dulcie had escaped long enough. I have heard things, too, and just lately. Dulcie is not the only one. She talked to Bess. Bess Walbert is as busy a little news circulator as you'd care to find."

"What did I tell you?" Natalie cried out in triumph.

"You were right, Nat. I give you credit for

reading her correctly. I haven't seen her since the first of the week. When I do——" Leslie nodded her head, looking thoroughly disagreeable. Elizabeth Walbert was in for a very stormy interview with her.

"When will you call the meeting, Les?" anxiously inquired Joan. "Don't put it off. No telling how much more mischief Dulcie may do if she isn't curbed promptly."

"Tomorrow night," Leslie named. See as many of the Sans as you can between now and the ten-thirty bell. Don't go near Loretta Kelly's and Della Byron's room. Dulcie goes there a good deal lately. Della is coming to see me this evening after dinner. I'll tell her then. Let me know before the last bell tonight how many of the girls are on, Nat. Will you?"

"Surely, Leslie dear." Natalie had simmered down to affability. She was very proud of Leslie's confidence in her.

Left alone, Leslie settled back in her chair very much as her father might have done on the eve of a pitched battle on the stock exchange. Her eyes roved about her room as she planned where the culprit should stand, where she wished the Sans to group themselves, and where her place as conductor of the arraignment should be.

A half smile flitted across her face as she remem-

bered the last high tribunal she had conducted.
This time the culprit was a real one. It had been
hard to trump up charges against "Bean." There
would be no masks worn save the mask of deceit
which she would ruthlessly strip from Dulcie, showing her in her true colors. After she was "all
through" with Dulcie she would read the riot act to
Bess Walbert. She wished to wait, however, until
the sophomore unsuspectingly came to her for a
favor. Then she would be shown a side of Leslie
she had not dreamed existed.

At twenty minutes after ten Natalie came to Leslie's room with the welcome news that "every last
Sans" except Loretta and Della had been told and
would be on hand promptly at eight o'clock the
next evening.

"I saw Loretta and Della," Leslie informed her
chum. "They are wild. They heard that Dulc told
two juniors about my renting that house for six
months so we could use it when we hazed Bean.
That's a nice report to have in circulation on the
campus, now isn't it? Does that sound like Dulc,
or doesn't it?"

"Dulcie told that, undoubtedly. There were not
more than six or seven of us who knew the terms
on which you rented that house. Dulc knew. You
always let her into extra private matters because
she was one of the old guard. You and she were

not so edgeways toward each other until after the night of the masquerade."

"We never agreed on a single thing. Away back at prep school Dulc and I were always squabbling. In her heart she has never really liked me. Since the masquerade she has cordially hated me. That's about my feeling toward her. I want her out of the Sans. She is a disgrace to them. I expected Nell Ray would fight for her, but she gave in as nicely as you please."

"The girls are all down on her for telling tales," returned Natalie. "I wonder if she thinks they don't know the way she has gossiped about them?"

"She will know it tomorrow night," asserted Leslie shortly.

"There goes the bell. I had better beat it. I have an hour's studying to do tonight yet, and I am so sleepy," Natalie yawned. "One thing more." Half way across the threshold she turned and re-entered the room. "How are you going to get Dulc on the scene?"

"Harriet is to tell her, late tomorrow afternoon, that the Sans are to meet in my room tomorrow night at eight to discuss something very important. She will come. She will be eaten up with curiosity to know what is going on. She'll be just a little bit surprised when she learns how much she has to do with that important discussion." Leslie threw back her head and laughed in her silent fashion.

"She deserves it." Natalie's whole face hardened perceptibly. "Look out for her, Les. She is capable of making a lot of fuss. We don't care to have Remson coming up here to see what the trouble is."

"If she is noisy, half a dozen of us will simply take her by the arms and bundle her off to her own room. It is only three doors from here," Leslie answered with cool decision. "I can manage her, I think."

The next day Dulcie received word of the meeting through the medium of Harriet. The latter delivered the notice in a careless tone which completely misled Dulcie.

"Why can't it be some place besides Leslie Cairns' room?" Dulcie pettishly demanded. "I hate to go near her!"

"Suit yourself," shrugged Harriet. "You can't say I didn't tell you about it. It won't be any place other than Leslie's room."

Her simulated indifference merely aroused in Dulcie a contrary resolve to attend that meeting at all costs. She had not been in Leslie's room since the opening of college. She had a curiosity to see what changes Leslie had made in it from the previous year. Strangely enough, her own misdeeds never crossed her mind. She had no thought, when regaling others with her chums' private affairs, that such treachery might possibly bring her a day of reckoning. The recent quarrels she had had with her former intimate, Eleanor Ray, and also Joan Myers, left no impression on her save a sullen dislike for the two girls because they had taken her to task for betraying their confidence.

As it was, she accepted an invitation to dinner at the Colonial extended her by Alida Burton. She lingered so long at the tea room that she walked into Leslie's room at ten minutes past eight.

Slow of comprehension, even she felt dimly the tension of the moment. The Sans sat or stood in little groups about the room. With her entrance, conversation suddenly languished and died out. Every pair of eyes was leveled at her in a cool fashion which bordered on hostility.

"It seems to me you are all very quiet tonight. What's the *matter?* Peevish because I'm late? *Yes? What?* Don't cry. Ten minutes won't kill any of you," she greeted flippantly. "Hope I haven't *missed* anything by being a tiny bit behind time." She had adopted Leslie's insolent swagger.

"No; you haven't missed anything," Leslie said dryly. "We were waiting for you." She turned abruptly from Dulcie, addressing the others.

"Girls," she raised her voice a trifle, "bring your

chairs and arrange them on each side of the daven-
port in a half circle.   Six girls can sit on the daven-
port.   We are all here now, so we can proceed with
the business of the evening."

Her order promptly obeyed, the Sans settled
themselves in their chairs with mingled emotions.
None of them had a definite idea of how Leslie intended to conduct the embarrassing session against
Dulcie.   Face to face with the momentous occasion,
a few of them felt slightly inclined toward clemency.   The older members of the Sans were too
greatly incensed by her treachery to do other than
approve of the humiliation about to descend on the
traitor.

It had been Leslie's first idea to seat Dulcie in a
particular chair.   Second thought assured her that
Dulcie would refuse the chair, merely to be contrary.   She would undoubtedly sit where she would
be most conspicuous if left to her own devices.   Leslie decided the rest of the Sans must sit in a com-
pact group.   Wherever Dulcie might choose to post
herself in the room she could not escape arraignment.

While the girls were arranging their chairs, Leslie occupied herself with hanging a heavy velvet
curtain in front of the door leading to the hall.
That task completed, she turned to find Dulcie had
seated herself on the left hand side of the semi-cir-

cle, the last girl in the row. She had pulled her chair forward a trifle so as to command a good view of the company.

Dulcie was well-pleased with herself. She was still admiring her brazen entrance into the room. She felt that she had quite outdone Leslie in matter of cool insolence. In fact she was much better able to direct the club than Leslie. She wondered the girls had never realized it. She eyed Leslie with ill-concealed contempt as the latter seated herself in the chair of office which Natalie had placed in the fairly wide space between the ends of the half circle. Les grew homelier every day, was her uncharitable opinion.

"We are here tonight to perform a duty, which, though not pleasant, *must be done.*" Leslie made this beginning with only a slight drawl to her tones. "When we organized the Sans Soucians we all promised to be loyal to one another. I regret to say that one of our number has so completely violated this promise it becomes necessary to take drastic measures. We cannot allow a Sans to betray deliberately either club or personal secrets."

Leslie placed great stress on "deliberately." She was careful not to look toward Dulcie. "Do you agree with me in this?" She put the question generally.

"*Yes,*" was the concerted, emphatic answer. Dulcie's voice helped to swell the chorus.

"The Sans have done certain things as a matter of reprisal and self-defense, which, if generally known, would entail very serious consequences. It is vital to our welfare at Hamilton that these matters should be kept secret, yet a member of the Sans has gossiped them to outsiders. For example, it is known to a number of seniors and juniors outside the Sans that a hazing affair took place last St. Valentine's night, conducted by the Sans. Seven of us have been approached on this subject. We know, to a certainty, that a faction, antagonistic to us, did not start this story.

"Still more serious is a report brought to me concerning the methods employed by Joan and I to keep a residence for the Sans at the Hall when we were threatened with expulsion from here as sophomores. A person who will betray such intimate matters, knowing that her treachery may ruin the prospects of her chums for graduation from college, is not only a fool for risking her own safety, but a menace to the club as well."

For ten minutes Leslie talked on in this strain, her hearers observing a strained silence. She was purposely piling up the enormity of Dulcie's misdeed so as to impress the others. As for Dulcie, she had begun to show signs of nervousness. Once

or twice her eyes measured the distance from her
chair to the door as if she were meditating sudden
flight. What remnants of conscience she still had,
stirred to the point of informing her that the coat
Leslie was airing fitted her too snugly for comfort.
She had not yet arrived at the moment of awaken-
ing, however. She believed Leslie's remarks to be
directed toward someone else. Margaret Wayne,
perhaps; or, Loretta Kelly. Leslie had once said
to her that Loretta was a gossip. Dulcie now tried
to recall an instance of Loretta's perfidy. It would
be to her interest to cite an instance of it should
Leslie call for special evidence. It would pay Loretta back for once having called her a stupid little
owl.

In the midst of racking her vindictive brain for
evidence against a fellow member, Dulcie lost briefly
the thread of Leslie's discourse. Mention of her
own name re-furnished her with it.

"Dulciana Vale," she heard Leslie saying in a
tense note quite different from her indolent drawl,
"do you know of any reason why you should be
allowed a further membership in the Sans Soucians
after having become an utter traitor to their interests?"

Dulcie struggled to her feet, her sulky features
a study in slow-growing rage. "What—what—do

you—mean?" Her voice was rising to a gasping scream. "How dare you call me a traitor. You are telling lies; just nothing but lies."

CHAPTER XIX

IN THE INTEREST OF PRIVATE SAFETY

"Sit down," ordered Leslie sharply, "and keep your voice down! You have made us all enough trouble. We don't propose that you shall add to it."

"I have not," shrieked Dulcie. "I don't know what you are talking about. You're crazy if you say I told all that stuff you mentioned. Why don't you put the blame where it belongs? You told me yourself that Loretta and Margaret were both gossips. You told Bess Walbert a lot of things yourself. She told me so. You used to tell Lola Elster a lot, too. Nat Weyman isn't above gossiping, either. She has said some *hateful* things about you, if you care to know it."

Fully launched, Dulcie bade fair to stir up dissension in a breath. Worse, her lung power seemed to increase with every word.

"Pay no attention to her," Leslie advised her

chums in a cold, level voice. "She can tell more yarns to the second than anyone else I know."

"You said you could manage her, Les. For goodness' sake do so. I am afraid she'll be heard down stairs." Joan Myers sprang to her feet in exasperation.

"Leave that to me." Leslie's eyes snapped. She was fast losing the admirable poise she had held so well. The real Leslie Cairns was coming to the surface.

Three or four lithe steps and she was facing Dulcie. The latter still stood by her chair shrieking forth invective.

"Listen to me, you *idiot*," she said with an intensity of wrath that approached a snarl. "Cut out that screaming—*now*. We are done with you. We know you for what you are. Not one of us will ever speak to you again after you leave this room. Get that straight. If you ever repeat another word on the campus of the Sans' business you will be a sorry girl. *Don't you forget that.* You carried the idea that, if trouble came from your talk, you could slide out of it and leave us to face it. You couldn't have cleared yourself. What you are to do from now on is——"

A sharp rapping at the door interrupted Leslie. Raising a warning finger to her lips, she crossed the room to answer the knock.

"Good evening, Miss Remson," she coldly greeted. "Will you come in? Our club is holding a meeting in my room." She made an indifferent gesture toward the assembled girls.

"Good evening, Miss Cairns. No; I do not wish to enter your room. I must insist, however, that you conduct your meeting quietly. The commotion going on in here can be heard downstairs."

The very impersonality of the manager's reproof brought a quick rush of blood to Leslie's cheeks. It was as though Miss Remson considered Leslie and her companions so far beneath her it took conscientious effort on her part even to reprove them. It stung Leslie to a desire to clear herself of the opprobrium.

"I am sorry about the noise," she apologized in annoyed embarrassment. "Miss Vale is responsible for it. I have been trying to quiet her. She is very angry with us for calling her to account for disloyalty. She has done so many despicable things we felt it necessary to call a meeting of the club to——"

"Pardon me. I am not interested in anything save the fact that there must be no more screaming or loud altercation from this room tonight or at any other time. As it is your room, Miss Cairns, I shall hold you responsible for the good behavior of your guests."

Again the aloofness of the rebuke cut Leslie

through and through. She had never believed that she could be so utterly snubbed by "Trotty" Remson.

"Very well." It was the only thing she could think of to say.

Miss Remson turned from the door and went on down the long hall. Leslie was seized with a savage inclination to bang the door. She refrained from indulging it. There had been enough noise already.

She returned to her companions to find Dulcie furious because she had been reported to Miss Remson as the author of the commotion.

"Talk about anyone being treacherous," she stormed, but in a more subdued key. *"You're* treacherous as a snake. *You'd* tell tales on—on your own father, if it would save you from disgrace."

"That's enough." Leslie's last atom of self-control vanished. "I am tired of your foolishness. Get out of my room, instantly. Don't you ever dare even speak to me again. Let me hear one word you have said against any of us and I will have you expelled within twenty-four hours afterward. I can do it, too. If you go to headquarters with any tales against us, remember you are one and we are seventeen who will act as one in denying your fairy stories. You——"

"Not fairy stories," sneered Dulcie. "I'd be satisfied to tell the truth about you deceitful things.
It would more than run you out of Hamilton.

"You couldn't tell the truth to save your life,"
retorted Leslie with a caustic contempt which hit
Dulcie harder than anything else Leslie had said
to her.

"I—I—think——" Dulcie struggled with her
emotions, then suddenly burst into hysterical sobs.
Her arm against her face to shut her distorted
features from sight of her accusers, she stumbled
to the door, groping for the knob with her free
hand. An instant and she had gone, too thoroughly
humiliated to slam the door after her. The sounds
of her weeping could be faintly heard by the others
until her own door closed behind her.

"Gone!" Joan Myers sighed exaggerated relief.

"Yes; and *broken*," announced Leslie Cairns
with cruel satisfaction.

"Oh, I don't know," differed Margaret Wayne.
She had not forgotten Dulcie's assertion as to what
Leslie had said of her and Loretta. "Dulc had
spunk enough to answer you back to the very last.
I don't see that——"

"No, you don't see. Well, I do. I say that
Dulcie Vale left here just now *utterly crushed*,"
argued Leslie with stress. "You are peeved, Mar-

garet, because of what she claimed I said of you and Retta. She lied."

"Certainly, Dulcie lied," supported Natalie. "Do you believe that *I*, Leslie's best friend, would say hateful things about her? Yet Dulc said I had. Didn't Les warn you not to pay any attention to what she said? We knew she would try to make trouble among the Sans the minute we called her down."

"We did, indeed." Leslie made a movement of her head that betokened Dulcie's utter hopelessness.

"I didn't say I believed what Dulcie said," half-apologized Margaret. In her heart she did not trust Leslie, however. It was like her to make just such remarks about any of the Sans if in bad humor.

"Never mind. It isn't worrying me," was the purposely careless response. "To go back to what you said about Dulc not being broken. I have known her longer than you, Margaret. She can keep up a row about so long, then she crumples. After that there isn't a spark of fight left in her. She always ends by a fit of crying, next door to hysterics. Isn't that true of her, Nat?"

Natalie nodded. "Yes; Dulcie will mind her own affairs now and keep her mouth closed for a long time to come."

"She's afraid of me," Leslie continued, her intonation harsh. "She doesn't know just the extent of my influence here."

"Could you truly have her expelled within twenty-four hours?" queried Harriet Stephens somewhat incredulously.

"You heard me say so. It would take a very slight effort to do that. I could wire my father, then——" Leslie paused, looking mysterious. "Sorry, girls, but I can't tell you any more than that. I'll simply say that my wonderful father's influence can remove mountains, if necessary. That's why I was so furious with that little sneak for daring even to mention his name."

"Could your father's influence save you from being expelled if different things you have done here were brought up against you?" demanded Adelaide Forman.

Leslie's eyes narrowed at the question. It was a little too searching for comfort. In reality her father's influence at Hamilton was a minus quantity. She had been boasting with a view toward increasing her own importance.

"It would depend entirely on what I had done," she answered after a moment's thought. "You must understand that my father would be wild if he knew I had gone out hazing when it is strictly against rules. He wouldn't do a thing to help me if I had trouble with Matthews over that. If I wrote him that Dulcie, for instance, was trying, by lies, to have me or my friends expelled from Hamilton, he would fight for me in a minute."

The Sans stayed for some time in Leslie's room planning how they would meet further remarks leveled at them on the campus as a result of Dulcie's defection. Leslie brought forth a fresh five-pound box of chocolates and another of imported sweet crackers. The party feasted and enjoyed themselves regardless of the fact that three doors from them a former comrade writhed and wept in an agony of angry shame. While in a measure their course might be justified, there was not one among them who had not, to a certain extent, and at some time or other, betrayed friendship.

This was also Dulcie's most bitter grievance against those who had been her chums. She knew now that she had talked too much. So had the others. Still, she was sorry for herself. She had been deceived in Bess Walbert. Bess was the one who had circulated most of the Sans' private affairs. She could not recall just how much she had told Bess; very likely no more than had Leslie. If they had given her time she would have been able to defend herself. With such reflections she strove to palliate her own offenses.

"Do you imagine Dulc will try to get back at us?" was Natalie's first remark to Leslie as the door closed on the departing Sans. "She carried on about as I thought she might. We came off easily with Remson, didn't we?"

"Dulcie is done, I tell you," re-asserted Leslie with an impatient scowl. "Remson! Humph! My worst enemy couldn't have delivered a more telling snub. She may suspect us of making trouble between her and Matthews. I'll say, I wish this year was done and Commencement here. If we slide through and capture those precious diplomas without the sword falling it will be a miracle."

CHAPTER XX

A BITTER PILL

DULCIE'S tumultuous resentment of accusation had been heard throughout the Hall. More than one door opened along the second, third and fourth story halls as the shrill-sounding voice continued.

Among others, Jerry had gone to the door to ascertain what was happening in the house of such an unusual nature. Two or three moments of intent listening and she had returned to her chair before the center table.

"Why waste my good time listening to the far-off scrapping of the Sans?" she had lightly questioned. "There is some kind of row going on in Miss Cairns' room. That's the way it sounds to me. I can't say who is giving the vocal performance. I don't know the dear creatures well enough to tag that sweet voice. I could hear other doors besides ours open. We are not alone in our curiosity."

"Your curiosity," Marjorie had corrected. "I wasn't enough interested to go to the door." Marjorie had laughed teasingly.

"Stand corrected. My curiosity," Jerry had obligingly answered. With that the subject had dropped as abruptly as the noise had begun.

The Sans were fortunate, in that the students residing at Wayland Hall, with the exception of themselves, were too fruitfully engaged in the minding of their own affairs to give more than a passing attention to the disturbance created by Dulcie Vale. Within the next two or three days they were agreeably surprised to find that no word of it had uttered on the campus.

"Has anyone said anything to you of Dulcie's roars, howls and shrieks?" Leslie asked Natalie, half humorously. It was the fourth evening after the meeting in her room and the two were lounging in Natalie's room doing a little studying and a good deal of talking.

"No. You can see for yourself what the girls in this house are; a mind-your-own-business crowd." Natalie's reply contained a certain amount of admiration. "If the story of it spreads over the campus, it will not be their fault. Sometimes I am sorry, Les, we didn't go in for democracy from the first. We are cut out of a lot of good times by being so exclusive. Take this show that Miss Page and Miss Dean are going to give in the gym tomorrow night. Not one of the Sans was asked to be in it."

"Hardly!" Leslie laughed and raised her eyebrows. "I can't imagine Bean doing anything like that."

"You needn't make fun of me. We couldn't expect to be asked to take part. I simply mentioned it as an example of the way things are. There is a great deal of sociability going on this year at Hamilton among the whole four classes, yet the Sans are as utterly out of it as can be," Natalie complained with evident bitterness.

"Glad of it," was the unperturbed retort. "Why yearn to be in a show, Nat, at this late stage of the game? Next winter, when you are in New York society, you'll have plenty of opportunity for amateur theatricals."

"Oh, I daresay I shall." This did not console Natalie. Of all the Sans, she was the only one not satisfied with her lot. She would not have exchanged places with any student outside her own particular coterie. Still, she had dreamed from her freshman year of shining as a star in college theatricals. To her lasting disappointment, she had never been invited to take part in an entertainment. The Sans had neither the inclination nor the ability to engineer a play or revue. The democratic element at Hamilton did not require the Sans' services.

"Are you going to that show?" Leslie cast a peculiar glance at her friend.

"I—well, yes; I bought a ticket." Natalie appeared rather ashamed of the admission. "Did you buy one?" she hastily countered.

"Yes; two. Laura Sayres bought them for me. Humphrey has them for sale in her office. I asked Laura if everything were just the same with Matthews since that Miss Warner substituted for her. She said all was O. K. She has her files, letters and papers arranged so that no one could ever make trouble for her."

"Too bad, Leslie, that Miss Warner was the one to substitute for Laura. It gave her a chance to meet Doctor Matthews. One never can tell what might develop from even so small an incident as that." Natalie was not disposed to be re-assuring that evening.

"Will you cut out croaking, Nat?" Leslie

sprang from her chair and began a nervous pacing of the floor. "You might as well pour ice-water down the back of my neck. Enough annoying things have happened lately to worry me without having to reckon on what 'might' happen. I told Sayres to take good care of herself and try not to be away from her position again. I advised her, if ever she had to be away, even for a day, to supply her own sub. She should have had sense enough to do so the last time."

"I am surprised that Miss Warner does secretarial work when that Miss Lynne she rooms with is wealthy in her own right," commented Natalie.

"I suppose that green-eyed ice-berg wants to earn her own money. I made a mistake about Lynne. Her father is the richest man in the far west. My father told me so last summer. I always meant to tell you that and kept on forgetting it. He said then I ought to be friends with her, but I told him 'nay, nay.' She and I would be *so pleased* with each other." Leslie smiled ironically.

" 'The richest man in the far west,' " repeated Natalie, her mind on that one enlightening sentence. "Too bad she isn't our sort. We could ask her into the Sans in Dulcie's place."

"She wouldn't leave Bean and Green-eyes and those two savages, Harding and Macy. I sometimes admire those two. They have so much nerve. Dulcie's place will stay vacant. I wouldn't ask Lola to join us after the way she has dropped me for Alida. As for Bess; she has yet to hear from me. I have an idea she and Dulc will get together. Dulc will tell her the news. Then Bess will sidle around me thinking she can get into the Sans. What? Watch my speed!" The corners of Leslie's mouth went down contemptuously. She was a match for the self-seeking sophomore.

The next evening being that of the revue, Leslie and Natalie attended it together. The rest of the Sans had elected also to go to it. Leslie had advised against going in a body. "If we do, they'll think we were anxious to see their old show," she had argued. "We'd better scatter by twos and threes about the gym."

By a quarter to eight the gymnasium was packed with students, faculty, and a goodly sprinkle of persons from the town of Hamilton who had friends among the students. Robin and Marjorie had worried for fear the programme might be too long. There would be sure to be encores. Their choice of talent, however, was so happy that the audience could not get enough of the various performers.

Marjorie was keyed up to the highest pitch of joy by the presence of Constance Stevens and Harriet Delaney. They had arrived from New York late that afternoon on purpose to take part in the show.

While the wonder of Constance's matchless high soprano notes in two grand opera selections awarded her a fury of applause, Harriet came in for her share of glory. It may be said that Constance and Veronica divided honors that evening.

Urged by Marjorie, Ronny had sent to Sanford for the black robe she used in the "Dance of the Night." It had been in her room in Miss Archer's house since the evening of the campfire three years before. Besides the "Dance of the Night" she gave a fine exhibition of Russian folk dancing in appropriate costume.

Marjorie had felt impelled to write Miss Susanna a special note of invitation inclosing several tickets. "Jonas or the maids might like our show, even if Miss Susanna won't come. Of course she won't, but I wanted her to have the tickets," she had said to Jerry, who had agreed that her head was level and her heart in the right place as usual.

For the first time since the beginning of her hatred for Hamilton College, Miss Susanna had been sorely tempted to break her vow and attend the show. Realizing the sensation her presence on the campus would create, she quickly abandoned the impulse. She was half vexed with Marjorie for sending her tickets and made note to warn her never to send any more.

Of all the audience, those most impressed by

performance and performers were the Sans. While
they enjoyed the revue, girl-fashion, as a spectacle,
the knowledge of the enemy's triumph was hard to
swallow. Ronny's dancing was a revelation to
them, astonishing and bitter. As each number appeared, perfect in its way, the realization of the
cleverness of the girls they had affected to despise
came home as a sharp thrust.

Leslie Cairns was particularly disgruntled as she
hurried Natalie from the gymnasium and into the
cold clear December night.

"Don't talk to me, Nat," she warned. "I am so
upset I feel like howling my head off. The way
Beanie has come to the front is a positive crime.
Did you see her marching around the gym tonight
as though she owned it?"

"It was a good show," Natalie ventured.

"Entirely too good," grumbled Leslie. "I don't
like to talk of it. Did I mention that Bess wrote
me a note. She wants to see me about something
very important." Leslie placed satirical stress on
the last three words. She may see me but she won't
be pleased. I'm in a very bad humor tonight. I
shall be in a worse one tomorrow."

CHAPTER XXI

"DISPOSING" OF BESS

LESLIE'S ominous prediction regarding herself was not idle. She awoke the next morning signally out of sorts. Though she had declared to Natalie she did not care to discuss the revue, when she arrived at the Hall she had changed her mind. She had invited Natalie into her room for a "feed." The two had gorged themselves on French crullers, assorted chocolates and strong tea. Nor did they retire until almost midnight.

Leslie greeted the light of day with a sour taste in her mouth and a desire to snap at her best friend, were that unlucky person to appear on her immediate horizon. She had thought herself fairly well prepared in psychology for the morning recitation. Instead she could not remember definitely enough of what she had studied the afternoon before to make a lucid recitation. This did not tend to render her more amiable. She prided herself particularly on her progress in the study of psychology and was inwardly furious at her failure.

Exiting from Science Hall that afternoon, the first person her eyes came to rest upon was Elizabeth Walbert. She stood at one side of the broad stone flight of steps eagerly watching the main entrance to the building.

"Oh, there you are!" she hailed. "I have been waiting quite a while for you."

"That's too bad." It was impossible to guage Leslie's exact humor from the reply. Her answers to impersonal remarks so often verged on insolence.

"So I thought," pertly retorted the other girl. At the same time she furtively inspected Leslie.

"What is it now? You make me think of that old story of the 'Flounder' in 'Grims' Fairy Tales.' You are like the fisherman's wife who was always asking favors of the flounder. We will assume that I am the flounder."

"How do you know that I wish to ask a favor?" Elizabeth colored hotly at the insinuation. She put on an injured expression, her lips slightly pouted.

"I'm a mind reader," was the laconic reply.

"Hm! Suppose I were to ask you to do something for me? Haven't you *said* lots of times that I could rely on you?" persisted Elizabeth. "I don't understand you, Leslie. You are so sweet to me at times and so horrid at others."

"You'll understand me better after today," came

the significant assurance. "Come on. We will walk across the campus to your house."

"Why not yours?" Elizabeth demanded in patent disappointment. "I see enough of Alston Terrace. I'd rather go with you to Wayland Hall. Your nice room is a fine place for a confidential chat."

"You won't see the inside of it this P. M. I am not going into the house when we come to Alston Terrace. I have a severe headache and choose to stay out in the open air. It's a fair day, and not cold enough to bar a walk on the campus."

"Very well." Elizabeth sighed and looked patient. "I hope we don't meet any of the girls. I have a private matter to discuss with you."

"Go ahead and discuss it," imperturbably ordered Leslie.

"Why—you—perhaps, if you have a headache, I had better wait until another time," deprecated the sophomore. It occurred to her that she ought to pretend solicitude. "I am so sorry," she hastily condoled.

"Thank you. There is no 'if' about my head-ache. Get that straight. What? It won't hinder me from listening to you. Let's hear your remarks now and have them over with."

"I have seen Dulcie," began Elizabeth impres-sively, "and she has told me what happened the other night. Really, Leslie, I was *shocked, simply*

shocked. Yet I couldn't blame you in the least.
The way Dulcie has talked about you on the campus
is disgraceful. But I went over all that with you
the day I first told you of how treacherous she had
been."

"Quite true. You did, indeed," Leslie conceded
with pleasant irony. "Now proceed. What next?"

"You are so *funny, Leslie.* You are so *deliciously*
matter-of-fact." Elizabeth was hoping the compli-
ment would restore the difficult senior to a more
equitable frame of mind.

"You may not always appreciate my matter-of-
fact manner." The ghost of a smile, cruel in its
vagueness, touched Leslie's lips.

"Oh, I am *sure* I shall. To go back to Dulcie, I
hope you didn't mention my name the other night.
You promised you wouldn't."

"Is that what you have been so anxious to tell
me?" Leslie asked the question with exaggerated
weariness, eyes turned indifferently away from her
companion.

"No; it is not." Elizabeth shot an exasperated
glance at her. "I merely mentioned it. Dulcie
tried to make me take the blame for it the first time
I met her after the meeting. I simply told her I
had nothing to do with it whatever."

Leslie sniffed audible contempt at this information. "Let me say this: Dulcie herself mentioned

your name, or rather she screamed it out at the top
of her voice the other night. The rest of us said
nothing. I made the charges against Dulcie and
mentioned no names."

"I wish I had been there." A wolfish light
flashed into the wide, babyish blue eyes. "It must
have been quite a party. Leslie," Elizabeth decided
that the time had come to speak for herself, "you
said once that I couldn't be a member of the Sans
because there was no vacancy; that the club must
be kept to the number of eighteen. There is a
vacancy *now*. The club has only seventeen members. Why can't I fill that vacancy and become the
eighteenth member? I don't mind because it will
be only for the rest of this year. I shall count it an
honor to have been a Sans even that long. I will
certainly make a more loyal Sans than Dulcie was."

Leslie drew a long breath. The wished-for
moment had come. She was in fine fettle to deliver
to the ambitious climber the "turn-down" she had
earned.

"Why can't you become a member of the Sans?"
she asked, then drew back her head and indulged in
soundless laughter. "Do you think it would make
you very happy to join us?"

"You may better believe it," Elizabeth made flip-
pant reply. More seriously, she added: "You know

how my heart has been set upon it from the very first."

"Yes, I know. The fact of the matter is," Leslie measured each word, "there is one great drawback to your joining."

"If it is about money, I am sure my father has as much as the fathers of the other members," cut in Elizabeth. "Our social position in New York is——"

"All that has nothing to do with the drawback I mentioned." Leslie waved away Elizabeth's attempt at defending her position. They were not more than half way across the campus, but Leslie was tired of keeping up the suspense of the moment. Her head ached violently. She was so utterly disgusted with the other girl she could have cheerfully pummeled her.

"Then I don't quite understand——" began Elizabeth.

"You're going to—at once. We dropped one girl from the Sans for being a liar and a gossip. What would be the use in filling her place with another liar and gossip. That's the drawback. It applies strictly to you."

Leslie stopped short in her walk and faced her companion, her heavy features a study in malignant contempt. Elizabeth's eyes widened involuntarily this time. She could not believe the evidence of her own ears. Her moment of stupefaction gave Leslie the very opportunity to continue and finish her remarks before the other had time for angry defense.

"You would have been nothing socially on the campus if I hadn't taken you up," she said forcefully. "The other girls in my club, it is my club, didn't like you. I had a good many quarrels with a number of them for trying to stand up for you, you worthless little schemer. If you had had one shred of principle or gratitude in your deceitful composition, you would have come to me at once with the first story against the club which Dulc told you. But you did not. You simply gossiped all she said to you to other students on the campus. Dulcie told you things about us that were ridiculous. You not only listened to them. You repeated them, making them worse.

"I had heard of your tactics before I sent for you to ask you about Dulc. I wanted to pump you and hear what you had to offer. I made it my business afterward to look up your record as a tale-bearer. Some little record! I know exactly to whom you have talked and what you have circulated concerning the Sans. You ought to be *ashamed* of yourself. Such ingrates as you have no sense of shame. Now, I believe, you understand why the Sans don't care to put you in Dulcie's place. It would merely be a case of out of the frying pan into the fire. Of the two, you are worse than Dulc. She is a liar, but stupid. You are a liar and tricky."

"Don't you *dare* call me a story-teller again," burst forth Elizabeth in a fury.

"I didn't say story-teller. I said liar. I never mince matters. I've said that to you before." Leslie stood smiling at the culprit, the soul of mockery.

"You won't be at Hamilton long enough to insult me ever again, Leslie Cairns," threatened Elizabeth, a world of vindictiveness in every word. "I don't believe you, when you say that Dulcie hasn't told the truth. I guess Dulcie knows enough that is true to make it very uncomfortable for you. I'll help her do it, too. No one can speak to me as you have and expect I won't get even."

"Try it," challenged Leslie. "Unless you have Dulcie to back you you can't prove one single thing against our record at Hamilton. Dulcie doesn't care to make trouble for herself. You couldn't get her to go with you to headquarters. She has either to be graduated from college with a fair rating or fall into a bushel of trouble with her father. Let me give you and Dulc both a last piece of advice. You'll tell her all about this, of course, only you will be careful not to mention wanting her place in the club. Keep a brake on those mill-clapper tongues of yours for the rest of the year."

Without giving Elizabeth time for another outburst of wrath, Leslie wheeled and started away at double quick. The other girl forgot dignity entirely, and pursued the senior, talking shrilly as she ran. She might as well have pursued a fleeing shadow. Leslie set her jaw and increased her pace. The enraged sophomore kept up the chase for a matter of yards, then stopped. Placing her hands to her mouth, trumpet fashion, she hurled after Leslie one pithy threat: "You'll be sorry."

CHAPTER XXII

PLANNING FOR THE FUTURE

THE approach of the Christmas holidays called a halt in the internal war which raged between the Sans and their two betrayers. Having delivered her ultimatum to Elizabeth Walbert, Leslie promptly proceeded to forget her, so far as she could. As a result of the tactics she had pursued with both Dulcie and Elizabeth, she was more at ease than for a long time. She was confident she had bullied both to a point where they would hesitate before doing any more idle talking about the Sans' misdemeanors. Every day which passed over her head without mishap to herself was one day nearer Commencement and freedom. She had no regret for her misdeeds. She was merely in fear lest they might be brought to light.

She had lost all interest in leadership at Hamilton. Her one idea now was to end her college course creditably and thus earn her father's approval. Natalie Weyman was on better terms with her than were the other Sans. They found her moody indifference harder to combat than her bullying. She was interested in nothing the club did or wished to do. "Go as far as you like, but let me alone," became her pet answer to her chums' appeals for advice or an expression of opinion.

"The Sans have become so exclusive they've nearly effaced themselves from the college map," Jerry remarked to Marjorie several days after their return from the Christmas vacation at home.

"They have had to settle down and do some studying, I presume," was Marjorie's opinion. "They used to be out evenings a good deal oftener than ever we were. I've wondered how they kept up at all."

"Leila said that Miss Vale had been conditioned two or three times, and had to hire a tutor to help pull her through. I notice she doesn't go around with any of the Sans. You remember I spoke of her having changed her seat at table the next day after that fuss up in Miss Cairns' room."

"I have seen her with Miss Walbert a good deal lately. It seems odd, Jeremiah, that, after all the trouble we had with those girls as freshies and sophs, we should be almost free of them this year. It has been such a beautiful, peaceful year, thus far. We've had the gayest, happiest kind of times. If only we could keep Leila, Vera, Kathie and Helen with us next year everything would be perfect."

"Would it? Well, I rather guess so. Gives me the blues every time I stop to think about losing them. Just when we are traveling along so pleasantly, too. Here we are, victorious democrats. We know Miss Susanna, even if we don't dare boast of it. We've been entertained at Hamilton Arms; something President Matthews can't say. You and Robin are successful theatrical managers. Oh, I can tell you, everything is upward striving.

" 'Tis as easy now for hearts to be true,
   As for grass to be green and skies to be blue.
   'Tis the natural way of living"

gayly quoted Marjorie, patting Jerry's plump shoulder in her walk across the room to find a pencil she had mislaid.

"I wish we would hear from Miss Susanna," she

continued, a little wistful note in the utterance.
Perhaps she did not like our Christmas remembrance. She doesn't like birthday observances.
She loves flowers, though. So she couldn't really
regard those we sent her as a present. And that
letter was delightful, I thought. We may have
made a mistake in sending the wreath."

The letter to which Marjorie referred was a composite. Each of the nine girls had contributed a
paragraph. They had tucked it into a box of long-
stemmed red roses which they had selected as a
Yule-tide offering to the last of the Hamiltons.
With it had gone a laurel wreath, to which was
attached a large bunch of double, purple violets.
They had asked that the wreath be hung in Brooke
Hamilton's study above the oblong which contained
the founder's sayings.

"I don't believe Miss Susanna is on her ear at
us," observed Jerry inelegantly. "She will write
when she feels like it. Maybe she thought it better
to postpone writing until she was sure we were all
back at college after Christmas. When did you last
hear from her?"

"Not since she sent me the money for the tickets
for the show. I bought those tickets for her myself. She didn't understand, I guess. I re-mailed
the money to her, explaining that they were from
me. Since then I have heard not a word from her.

I should have taken the tickets back to her instead
of mailing them, but I was so busy just then. Besides, I don't like to go to the Arms without a
special invitation."

Almost incident with Marjorie's worry over Miss
Susanna's silence came a note from her new friend,
appointing an evening for her to dine at Hamilton
Arms.

"I am not asking your friends this time," the old
lady wrote, "as I prefer to devote my attention to
you, dear child. I could not answer the Christmas
letter for I had no medium of expression. I loved it,
and the flowers. Best of all, was the honor you
did Uncle Brooke. You may show this letter to
your friends, extending to them a crabbed old person's sincere thanks and good wishes."

Marjorie kept her dinner appointment with Miss
Susanna and spent a happy evening with the old
lady. Miss Hamilton showed active interest in the
subject of the recent revue. The obliging lieutenant had brought with her a programme which the
old lady insisted in going over, number by number,
inquiring about each performer. She expressed a
wish to hear Constance Stevens sing and asked
Marjorie to bring Constance to Hamilton Arms if
she should again come to Hamilton College.

"I was truly sorry to have missed that show,"
the last of the Hamiltons frankly confessed. It

would never do for me to set foot on that campus.
I should be on bad terms with myself forever after;
on as bad terms as I am with the college."

"I'll tell you what we might do, Miss Hamilton,"
Marjorie ventured. "We could give a stunt party
here, just for you, at some time when it pleased
you to have us here. Perhaps Constance would
come from New York for a day or two. She isn't
so far away. Then Ronny and Vera would dance
and Leila sings the most charming ancient Celtic
songs."

Her lovely face had grown radiant as she de-
scribed her chums' talents, and again, for her sake,
Miss Susanna had softened toward all girlhood.
She had assented with only healf-concealed eagerness to Marjorie's plan.

Two days after Marjorie's visit to her, she sent
her a check for five hundred dollars, asking that it
be placed with the money earned from the revue.
The youthful managers had charged a dollar apiece
for tickets with no reservations. To their intense
joy and amusement, the gross receipts amounted to
six hundred and seventy-two dollars. Their only
expenses being for printing and lighting the gymnasium, they had, counting Miss Susanna's gift, a
little over one thousand dollars with which to start
the beneficiary fund.

Anna Towne had done good work among the

girls off the campus. Due to her efforts they had been brought to look upon the new avenue of escape from signal discomfort, now open to them, as an opportunity to be embraced. Marjorie had said conclusively that the funds at their disposal were to be given, not lent. She argued on the basis that money thus easily gained should be distributed where it would benefit most, then be forgotten. The girls who were struggling along to put themselves through college would have enough to do to earn their living afterward without stepping over the threshold of their chosen work saddled with an obligation.

It took tact, delicacy and more than one friendly argument to establish this theory among the sensitive, proud-spirited girls for whose benefit the project had been carried out. Gradually it gained ground and a new era of things began to spring up for those who had sacrificed so much for the sake of the higher education. The money so easily earned by Ronny's nimble feet, Constance's sweet singing and the talent of the other performers revolutionized matters in the row of cheerless houses, in one of which Anne Towne resided. Ability to pay a higher rate for board brought better food and heat. The drudgery of laundering was lifted, the work being intrusted to several capable laundresses in the vicinity. Those who had kept house aban-

doned cooking and took their meals at one or another of the boarding houses. According to Anna
Towne, the restfulness of the changed way of living was unbelievable.

As successful theatrical managers, Robin and
Marjorie had rosy visions of a dormitory built
where several of the dingy boarding houses now
stood. Perhaps by next year they would have the
means to buy the properties. They purposed agi-
tating the subject so strongly, during their senior
year, that, at least, a few of the students among the
other three classes would be willing to go on with
the work.

Both had agreed that they had set themselves a
hard row to hoe, yet neither would have relinquished the self-imposed task. In the first flush of
their ambition they had asked Miss Humphrey to
ascertain, if she could, whether the regulations of
the college forbade the erection of more houses on
the campus. She had returned the answer, that,
owing to a peculiar will left by Mr. Brooke Hamilton, the consent to build on the campus would have
to come from Miss Hamilton, who had been preju-
diced against Hamilton College for many years.

This was a disturbing revelation to Marjorie.
She was fairly certain that Miss Susanna would
never give any such consent. She therefore

promptly abandoned the idea and laid her plans for the outside territory.

As the winter winged away Marjorie made more than one visit to Hamilton Arms. Occasionally her chums accompanied her. The Nine Travelers gave their stunt party at the Arms on Saint Valentine's eve. To please their lonely hostess they dressed in the costumes they intended wearing at the masquerade the next evening. Constance and Harriet managed to get away from the conservatory for three days, and a merry party ate a six o'clock dinner with Miss Susanna so as to have plenty of time for the stunts afterward.

Discreet to the letter, their visits to Hamilton Arms were known to no one outside their own group. Over and over again, when alone with the old lady, she would say to Marjorie: "I had no idea girls could be honorable. I had always considered boys far more honest and loyal."

"You and Miss Susanna Hamilton are getting very chummy, aren't you?" greeted Jerry, as Marjorie sauntered into their room one clear frosty evening in March, after having had tea at Hamilton Arms.

"I don't know whether we are or not." A tiny pucker decorated Marjorie's forehead. "I always feel a little uncertain of how to take her. She is kindness itself, then, all of a sudden, she turns crotchety and says she hates everything and everybody. Then she generaly adds, 'Don't take that to yourself, child.' "

"She thinks a lot of you or she wouldn't be so friendly with you. She looks at you in the most affectionate way. I've noticed it every time we have been to the Arms with you."

"I am glad of it. I was fond of her before I met her. Captain would like her. So would your mother, Jeremiah. Next year when our mothers come to Hamilton to see us graduate, I hope Miss Susanna will like to meet them. Only one more year after this. Oh, dear! I do love college, don't you?" Marjorie began removing her hat and coat, an absent look in her brown eyes.

"I have seen worse ranches," Jerry conceded with a grin. "Speaking of ranches reminds me of the West. The West reminds me of Ronny. Ronny promised to help me with my French tonight. Mind if I leave you? Such partings wring the heart; mine I mean. You go gallavanting off to tea with no regard for my feelings." Jerry gave a bad imitation of a sob, giggled, and began gathering up her books.

"I'll try to have more consideration for your feelings hereafter," Marjorie assured, a merry twinkle in her eyes.

"I'll believe that when I see signs of reform," Jerry threw back over her shoulder as she exited.

Left alone, Marjorie tried to shut out the memory of Hamilton Arms and settle down to her studying. The fascination of the old house held for her remained with her long after she had left it behind her on her now fairly frequent visits there. Nicely launched on the tide of psychology, an uncertain rapping at the door startled her from her absorption of the subject in hand. It flashed across her as she rose to answer the knocking that it had been done by an unfamiliar hand. None of the girls she knew rapped on the door in that weak, hesitating fashion.

As she swung open the door she made no effort to force back the expression of complete astonishment which she knew had appeared on her face. Her caller was Dulcie Vale.

CHAPTER XXIII

AN AMAZING PROPOSAL

"I—ARE you alone, Miss Dean? I would like to talk with you, but not unless you are alone." Dulcie spoke just above a whisper, peering past Marjorie into the room so far as she could see from where she was standing.

"Yes, I am alone. Miss Macy will not be back for an hour, perhaps. Will you come in, Miss Vale?" Marjorie endeavored to make the invitation courteous. She could not feign cordiality.

"I am glad you are alone." This idea seemed uppermost in Dulcie's mind. "I know you don't like me, Miss Dean. You haven't any reason to after the way you were treated by the Sans last Saint Valentine's night. Of course, I know you know who we were that night." She paused, as though considering what to say next.

"I saw no faces, but I knew Miss Cairns' and Miss Weyman's voices," Marjorie said with a suspicion of stiffness. She was not pleased to hear Dulcie preface her remarks with implied aspersions against the Sans. She knew that the latter had quarreled with her. She guessed that pique might have actuated the call.

"You never told anyone a single thing about it, did you?" The question was close to wistful. It seemed remarkable to Dulcie that Marjorie could have kept the matter secret.

"No." Marjorie shook her head slightly.

"Did your friends ever say a word about it? Those were your friends who burst in on us and made such a noise, weren't they? Who was the one who looked so horrible and blew out the candles?" Dulcie seemed suddenly to give over to curiosity.

"I can't answer your questions, Miss Vale." Marjorie could not repress the tiny smile that would not stay in seclusion. "I wish you would sit down and tell me frankly why you came to see me. You have not been in my room since the night of my arrival at Wayland Hall as a freshman."

"I know." Dulcie's gaze shifted uneasily from Marjorie's face. "I thought I would come again," she excused, "but——"

The steadiness of Marjorie's eyes forbade further untruth. She became suddenly silent. Very humbly she accepted the chair her puzzled hostess shoved forward. Marjorie sat down in one at the other side of the center table.

"I suppose you've heard all about my trouble

with the Sans," the visitor commenced afresh and awkwardly. "I don't belong to the Sans Soucians now. I wouldn't stay in a club with such dishonorable girls. I simply made Leslie Cairns accept my resignation. She was wild about it."

Now safely launched upon her story, Dulcie began to gather up her self-confidence. "You see, my father, who is president of the L. T. and M. Railroad, has done a great deal for the Sans. You know we have always come to Hamilton in the fall in his private car. I have lent the Sans money and done them endless favors, yet they couldn't be even moderately square with me." She fixed her eyes on Marjorie after this outburst as though waiting for sympathy.

"I have heard nothing in regard to your having left the Sans Soucians. I have noticed that you were no longer at the table where you formerly sat at meals." Marjorie could not honestly concede less than this.

"Didn't you hear us fussing one night in Leslie's room? It was before Christmas. That was the night I called them all down. I was so angıy! I went into a perfect frenzy! I'm so temperamental! When I am *really* in a rage it simply shakes me from head to foot." There was a faint impetus toward complacency in the statement.

"Yes; I heard a commotion going on up there

one evening, but only faintly. My door was closed. I didn't pay any attention to the noise, for it did not concern me." Marjorie was struggling against an irresistible desire to laugh. To her mind Dulcie was the last person she would have classed as temperamental.

"The rest of that crowd were just as noisy as I, but Leslie Cairns blamed me for it all. She told Miss Remson it was I alone who made the disturbance. I'll never forgive her; *never*. What I thought was this, Miss Dean. The Sans deserve to be punished for hazing you. I was a victim, too, that night. They made me go along with them, and I didn't wish to go. I came home with my eye blackened. I won't say how it happened, only that Leslie Cairns was to blame. I know about the whole plan for the hazing. Leslie rented that house for six months and paid the rent in advance so as to have a good place to take you. She would have left you there all night but Nell Ray and I said we would not stand for that. We were the only ones who stood up for you. Leslie Cairns was the Red Mask.

"You know that Doctor Matthews is awfully down on hazing," Dulcie continued, taking a fresh supply of breath. "I thought if you would go with me to his office we could put the case before him. So long as I have all the facts of that affair and you and I were the ones hazed, he would certainly expel those Sans from Hamilton. You could say, just to clear me, that you knew I was hazed, too. That is, I was forced to go with them against my will. You see I had said I wouldn't have a thing to do with it. I put on a domino that night over my costume and started across the campus by myself. Half a dozen of the Sans headed me off and simply dragged me along with them. I couldn't get away from them, either. If that wasn't hazing, then what was it?"

Marjorie was sorely tempted to reply, "Nothing but a yarn." She did not credit Dulcie's story and was growing momentarily more disgusted with the author of it.

"I can get away with it nicely if you will help me." Dulcie evidently took Marjorie's silence as favorable to her plan. "I've resigned from the Sans of my own accord. That will be in my favor. Matthews doesn't like Leslie. You know she received a summons after Miss Langly was hurt. Maybe the doctor didn't call her down! With you on my side. Oh, *fine!* I can see the Sans packing to leave Hamilton in a hurry!" Dulcie brightened visibly at the dire picture her mind had painted of her enemies' disaster. "I can tell you a lot more things against them, too. Leslie is afraid all the time that

Miss Remson will find out how she worked that stunt to keep us our rooms here. She——"

Marjorie interrupted with a quick, stern: "Stop, Miss Vale! I don't wish to hear such things. I listened to what you said about the hazing as that concerned myself only. I have no desire to know the Sans' private affairs. Whatever they may have done that is against the rules and traditions of Hamilton they will have to answer for. In the long run they will not be happy. I would not inform against them to President Matthews or anyone else."

"Would you let them go on and be graduated after what they have done against both of us?" demanded Dulcie, her voice rising.

"It has not hurt me; being hazed, I mean," was the calm reply. "I do not approve of hazing. I would not take part in any such disgraceful thing. Still, I do not believe in tale-bearing. You will gain more, Miss Vale, by going on as though all that has annoyed and hurt you had never been. Whoever has wronged you will be punished, eventually. The higher law, the law of compensation, provides for that."

"I don't know a thing about law. I wouldn't care to take the matter into court." Marjorie's little preachment had gone entirely over the stupid senior's head. Leslie had often remarked, and with truth, that Dulc was "thick."

"I mean by the higher law, 'As ye mete it out to others, so shall it be measured back to you again,' " Marjorie quoted with reverence.

"Oh, I see. You mean what the Bible says. Uh-huh! That's true, I guess." Dulcie looked vague. "I'm sorry you won't help me, Miss Dean. I feel that Doctor Matthews ought to *know* what's going on, when it is as serious as hazing."

Marjorie felt her patience winging away. She wished Jerry would suddenly return and thus end the interview. It was evident Dulcie intended to report the hazing, despite her refusal to become a party to the report. That meant she would be dragged into the affair.

"I wish you would not go to Doctor Matthews about the hazing, Miss Vale," she said abruptly. "If I, who was put to more inconvenience than you by it, have never reported it, I see no reason why you should. If you should succeed in having your former chums expelled you would feel miserably afterward for having betrayed them, no matter how much they might have deserved it."

"I surely should not." Dulcie's short upper lip lifted in scorn. "I would love to see them disgraced. They tried to down me. I have a splendid case against them because you are so well-liked on the campus. The use of your name will be of great help. Sorry you won't stand by me. You'll have to admit the truth if you are sent for at the office," she ended as a triumphant afterthought.

Marjorie contemplated her visitor in some wonder. The small, mean soul of the vengeful girl stood forth in the smile that accompanied her threatening utterance. It seemed strange to the upright lieutenant that a young woman with every material advantage in life could be so devoid of principle.

"Do not count on me." Marjorie's reply rang out with deliberate contempt. "If I were to be summoned to Doctor Matthews' office concerning the hazing, I would answer no questions and give no information."

This time it was Dulcie who lost patience. She rose with an angry flounce. Sulkiness at being thus thwarted replaced her earlier attempt at amenability.

"I might have known better than ask you," she sputtered, giving free rein to her displeasure. "I shall do just as I please about going to Matthews. I hope he sends for you. He will make you admit you were hazed by the Sans. Goodnight." She switched to the door. Her hand on the knob, she called over one shoulder: "I don't blame Les for having named you 'Bean.' You are just about as stupid as one."

CHAPTER XXIV

"THERE'S MANY A SLIP"

DULCIE'S parting fling drove away Marjorie's righteous indignation. It was so utterly childish. She smiled as she arranged her books and papers to her mind and sat down to study. Two or three times in the course of study the remark re-occurred to her and she giggled softly. The name 'Bean,' as applied to her by Leslie Cairns, had invariably made her laugh whenever she had heard it.

When Jerry finally put in an appearance, Lucy and Ronny at her heels, Marjorie related to them the incident of Dulcie's call.

"Oh, oh, oh!" groaned Jerry. "Why wasn't I here? I always miss the most exciting moments of life."

"I wished with all my heart that you would walk in and end the interview. She had so little honor about her I felt once as though I couldn't endure having her here another minute. Then she took herself off so suddenly I was amazed."

"Do you think she will go to Doctor Matthews?" Ronny asked rather skeptically. "Possibly what you said will take hold on her after all."

"No. She will go," Marjorie predicted with conviction. "She is determined on that. Maybe not right away. Goodness knows how much trouble it will stir up."

"You're right," nodded Jerry. "Bring the Sans to carpet and they will probably name us as the crowd who broke in on their ridiculous tribunal. What then?"

"If we are accused of any such thing we can only tell the truth," smiled Lucy. "We were in our masquerade costumes. We weren't wearing dominos, but our own coats and scarfs. We went to rescue Marjorie. We were not out on a hazing expedition."

"The only thing we should not have done, perhaps, was to blow out the candles," declared Ronny with a reminiscent chuckle. "That was my doing. Some of the Sans might have been quite seriously hurt in the dark. They deserved the few bumps they garnered. I'm not sorry for that part of our rescue dash on them."

"What a wonderful time we'll have if we are brought up to face the Sans in Doctor Matthews' office. Lead me to it; away from it, I had better say." Jerry made a wry face.

"Don't worry. I shall be on outpost duty," laughed Lucy. "I am going to begin substituting for the Doctor tomorrow morning. Miss Humphrey sent for me after biology this P. M. to ask me if I would. Miss Sayres has bronchitis. I am so far ahead in my subjects I can spare two weeks to the doctor's work. I was at Lillian's house for dinner tonight, so I didn't have a chance to tell you girls the news. If this affair comes up while I am working for the doctor, I shall no doubt hear of it. So long as we are all concerned in it, I shall feel I have the right to tell you if Miss Vale starts trouble."

The Lookouts were not in the least worried over their own position in the matter. While they might not escape reprimand, they had done nothing underhanded nor disgraceful. According to Jerry they had "sprung a beautiful scare where it was needed."

During the first week of her secretaryship for the doctor, Lucy heard nothing that would indicate the promised exposé on Dulcie's part. They saw her several times on the campus or driving with Elizabeth Walbert, apparently well pleased with herself. It was Jerry's opinion that she had built upon Marjorie's aid. Being denied this, she had abandoned the project as too risky to undertake alone.

One thing lynx-eyed Lucy discovered concerning

the secretary was her extreme carelessness in filing. More than once the doctor's patience and her own were taxed by protracted hunts on her part for correspondence on file.

"I exonerate you from blame for this, Miss Warner," the kindly doctor declared more than once. "I have spoken to Miss Sayres of this fault. I shall take it up with her again when she returns."

As the first week merged into the second and the second into the third, and still Lucy remained as the doctor's secretary, the two began to be on the best of terms. Quick to appreciate Lucy's remarkable brilliancy as a student, not to mention her perfect work as secretary, the doctor and she had several long talks on biology, mathematics, and the affairs of Hamilton College as well.

During one of these talks a gleam of light shone for a moment on the mystery Lucy never gave up hoping to solve. In mentioning Wayland Hall, the president referred to Miss Remson as one of his oldest friends on the campus.

"I have not seen Miss Remson for a very long time," he said with a slight frown. "Let me see. It will be——can it be possible?——two years in June. And she living so near me! She used to be a fairly frequent visitor at our house. I must ask Mrs. Matthews to write her to dine with us soon. Kindly remind me of that, Miss Warner; say this

afternoon before you leave. I will make a note
of it."

Lucy reminded him of the matter that afternoon
with a glad heart. She confided it to her Lookout
chums and they rejoiced with her. She would have
liked to tell Miss Remson the good news but courtesy forbade the doing. The Lookouts agreed
among themselves that it showed very plainly who
was responsible for the misunderstanding.

At the beginning of the fourth week Miss Sayres
returned. Lucy could only hope that Doctor Matthews had not forgotten to remind his wife of the
dinner invitation. She was sure, had Miss Remson
received it, that she would have mentioned it to
them. She would have wished the Nine Travelers
to know it. Whether Miss Remson would have
accepted it was a question. She had her own
proper pride in the matter. The girls had agreed
that should she mention it, Lucy was then to tell
her of the conversation with Doctor Matthews.

"Queer, but Miss Remson hasn't said a word
about receiving that invitation," Ronny said to
Lucy one evening shortly before the closing of college for the Easter holidays. "The doctor must
have forgotten all about it. That shows his conscience is clear. It would appear that he doesn't
even suspect Miss Remson has a grievance against
him."

"I am sure he forgot it." Lucy looked rather gloomy over the doctor's omission. "It was such a fine opportunity, and now it's lost. If I should work for him again I might remind him of it. If I did, I'd do more than mere reminding. I'd ask him to try to see Miss Remson and tell him I thought there had been a misunderstanding. I would have said so this time, but when he spoke of inviting her to their house for dinner, I supposed the tangle would be straightened post haste."

"He may happen to recall it months from now," Ronny consoled. "That's the way my father does. Men of affairs hardly ever forget things for good. Sooner or later a memory of that kind crops up again."

While Lucy worried because the doctor had forgotten his kindly intention toward their faithful elderly friend, Leslie Cairns was plunged in the depths of apprehension because of Lucy's substitution for Laura Sayres. Each day she wondered if the sword would fall. She visited Laura and made her worse by her irritating questions regarding the secretary's methods of filing. Was there any danger of old Matthews going through the files himself? Was Laura sure that she had eliminated every bit of evidence against them? Was she positive she had destroyed the letter Miss Remson had written him, supposedly? Nor had Leslie any mercy on the secretary's weakened condition. Laura bore her unfeeling selfishness without much protest. Leslie had given her one hundred dollars in her first visit. This palliated the senior's faults.

When at the end of the third week nothing had occurred of a dismaying nature, Leslie began to believe that her college career was safe. With Easter just ahead, a very late Easter, too, only two months stretched between her and Commencement, that dear day of honor and freedom for her. She had worried but little over Dulcie's threats. Elizabeth Walbert's parting shot, "You'll be sorry," crossed her mind occasionally. She attached not much importance to it at first and less as winter drew on toward spring.

Dulcie Vale, however, was only biding her time. She never relinquished for an hour her resolve to bring disgrace upon the Sans. Leslie having ordered her chums to steer clear of Bess Walbert, the latter also burned for revenge. She and Dulcie, after one glorious quarrel over what each had said about the other to Leslie, had made up and joined forces. They had a common object. Thus they clung together. They made elaborate plans for retaliation, only to abandon them for the one great plan, the betrayal of the Sans to Doctor Matthews.

Dulcie had at first decided to go to the president of Hamilton College within a few days after her unsuccessful talk with Marjorie. Then she thought of something else which pleased her better. She would wait until after Easter. If the Sans were expelled from college just before Easter, they would endeavor to slip away quietly, making it appear that they had left of their own accord. If she waited until they had returned, the blow would be far more crushing.

Regarding herself, Dulcie had her own plans. Her family, including her father, were in Europe. Her mother would not return until the next July. Her father, luckily for her, was to be in Paris until the following January. Her mother allowed her to do as she pleased. What Dulcie intended to do to please herself was to leave Hamilton on the Easter vacation not to return. She was not too stupid to realize that the Sans, accused of many faults by her, would turn on her *en masse* and implicate her. She could not hold out against them if arraigned in the presence of Doctor Matthews. She was also too heavily conditioned to graduate, and she hated college since her ostracization by the Sans. She was more than ready to leave. She would walk out and let her former chums bear the consequences. They had not spared her. She would not spare them.

CHAPTER XXV

WHEN THE SWORD FELL

THE longer Dulcie pondered the matter, the more she became convinced she could do more damage by letter than to go to the doctor in person. Elizabeth Walbert had several times advised this course. The latter knew nothing of Dulcie's resolve to leave college. Dulcie did not purpose she should until she wrote the sophomore from her New York apartment after leaving Hamilton. She had planned to take an apartment in an exclusive hotel on Central Park West. From there she would write her mother that she was too ill to return to college. She left it to her mother's tact to break the news to her father. He was not to know she had failed miserably in all respects at Hamilton.

Over and over again she wrote the damaging letter to Doctor Matthews. She wrote at first at length, putting in everything she could think of against the Sans. She made effort to stick to facts. There were enough of them to create havoc. Then she rewrote the letter, eliminating and revising until the finished product of her spite was worded to suit her. It was necessarily a long letter and could not fail in its object.

When college closed for Easter, Dulcie shook the dust of Hamilton from her feet and took her letter to New York with her. She did not inform the registrar that she would not return. She would write that from New York. The day after college reopened, following the ten days' vacation, Dulcie mailed four letters. One to Elizabeth Walbert, one to Miss Humphrey, one to Leslie Cairns, and *the* letter.

Those four letters created amazement, displeasure, consternation, according to the recipient. Miss Humphrey was annoyed as only a registrar can be annoyed by such a procedure. Elizabeth Walbert was surprised and miffed because Dulcie had not confided in her. Doctor Matthews' indignation soared to still heights. Leslie Cairns opened her letter at the breakfast table. She read the first page and hurriedly rose, tipping over her coffee in her haste. Paying no attention to the stream of coffee which flowed to the floor, she rushed from the dining room to her own. Locking the door, she sat down with trembling knees to read the letter. She read it twice, uttered a half sob of agony and threw herself face downward on her bed. The sword had fallen, the end had come.

Of the four letters, the one Dulcie had written her was the shortest and read:

"LESLIE:

"When you read this you will not feel so secure as you did the night you humiliated me so. You thought I would not dare say a word about a number of things because I was afraid of being expelled from college. You will see now that you made a serious mistake; so serious you won't be at Hamilton long after President Matthews receives the letter I have written him. I have told him *everything*. The Sans are in for trouble with him. It doesn't make a particle of difference to me what happens to you and your pals, for I am not coming back to Hamilton. My letter to Doctor Matthews is convincing. You will surely receive a summons. What? Oh, yes! I think I have proved myself almost as clever as you.

"DULCIANA MAUD VALE."

Not far behind Leslie came Natalie Weyman to her friend's room. Startled by Leslie's peculiar behavior she had followed her upstairs, her own breakfast untouched.

"Leslie," she called softly, "May I come in? It's Nat."

"Go away." Leslie's voice was harsh and

broken. "Come back after recitations this afternoon."

"Very well." Natalie retreated, puzzled but not angry. She was understanding that something very unusual had happened to Leslie. Her mind took it up, however, as presumably bad news from home. She hoped nothing serious had happened to Leslie's father. Her shallow serenity soon returned and she went about her affairs smugly unconscious of what was in store for her.

Meanwhile, President Matthews was holding a long and unpleasant session with Laura Sayres. Dulcie had not failed to describe Laura's part in the plot against Miss Remson. Now the incensed doctor was endeavoring to pin his shifty secretary down to lamentable facts.

Laura had always assured Leslie she would never divulge the Sans' secrets under pressure. For a short period only she lied, evaded and pretended ignorance. Little by little the ground was cut from under her treacherous feet. Before the morning was over President Matthews had the complete story of the trickery which had brought misunderstanding between him and Miss Remson. Of the hazing Laura knew little; enough, however, to establish the truth of Dulcie's confession.

"I have yet to find a more flagrant case of dishonorable dealing," were the doctor's cutting words at the close of that painful morning. "I trusted you. Knowing that, you should have been above trading upon my confidence. I cannot comprehend your object in allying yourself with these lawless young women. You say you are not a member of their club. Why, then, were their dishonest interests so dear to you?"

To this Laura made no reply save by sobs. She had crumpled entirely. One thing only she had rigorously kept back. She would not admit that she had been paid by Leslie Cairns for her ignoble services. If the doctor suspected this he made no sign of it. He dismissed her with stern brevity and was glad to see her go. Aside from her worthless character, she had not been a satisfactory secretary.

Immediately she was gone, he put on his hat and overcoat and set out for Wayland Hall. To right matters with his old friend was to be his second move.

Arriving at the Hall at the hour the students were returning for luncheon, his appearance caused no end of private flutter. Having, as yet, held no communication with Leslie, the older members of the Sans were thrown into panic, nevertheless. What they had least desired had come to pass. The Lookouts, on the contrary, were overjoyed. Helen

During the afternoon Leslie had received a telephone call from Laura Sayres. Laura had refused to go into much detail over the telephone. She announced herself as having been discharged from the doctor's employ and asserted that he knew "all about everything" without her having said a word of betrayal. Leslie had not stopped to consider whether she believed the secretary's story or not. She had said: "You can't tell me anything. I know too much already. Goodbye." With that she had hung up the receiver. Her eyes blinded by tears of defeat and real fear, she had stumbled her way to her room. There she had spent the most unhappy afternoon of her life.

"It's no use, girls. We are done. You may as well be thinking what excuse you can make to your families, for you will be expelled as sure as fate. Matthews' call on Remson shows that Dulcie betrayed us. Sayres was fired by the doctor; all on account of that Remson mix-up. She didn't see Dulcie's letter, but I know he received it. Sayres called me on the 'phone."

"But, Leslie, some of us don't know a thing about how you worked that Remson affair! You never told us. I don't see why we should be expelled for something we know nothing of." Eleanor made this half tearful defense.

"Oh, that isn't *all*." Leslie's loose-lipped mouth curled in a bitter smile. "There is the hazing business, too. Dulc told that, of course. Perhaps she told the 'soft talk' stunt Ramsey taught the soph team last year. I don't know. All is over for us. I do know that. I expected to go into business with my father after I was graduated from Hamilton. Now!" She walked away from her companions and stood with her back toward them at the window.

"Perhaps it will blow over," ventured Margaret Wayne. "I shall make a hard fight to stay on at Hamilton. I won't be cheated out of my diploma, if I can help it. It's our word against Dulcie's."

"That's of no use to us now." Leslie turned suddenly from the window with this gloomy utterance. "Remember Laura Sayres has been discharged from Matthews' employ. Remson and Matthews have had an understanding. What chance have we? Sayres told me the doctor quizzed her for over two hours. She claims she told nothing against us. I know better. If Dulcie, the little wretch, had sprung this before Easter we might have saved our faces. She waited purposely. She and Walbert deliberately planned this exposé. Look for a summons soon. We won't escape. I shall begin to pack tonight. So far as this rattletrap old college is concerned, I don't care a rap about leaving it. All that is worrying me is: What shall I say to my father?"

CHAPTER XXVI

MAY DAY EVENING

For two days, in a second floor class room at Hamilton Hall, a real tribunal, consisting of Doctor Matthews and the college Board, convened. Very patiently the body of dignified men listened to what the offenders against Hamilton College had to say by way of confession and appeal for clemency. To her great disgust, Marjorie was summoned before the Board on the morning of the second day. Questioned, she admitted to having been hazed. More than that she refused to state.

"I claim the right to keep my own counsel," she had returned, when pressed to relate the details of the incident. "I was not injured. I did not even contract a slight cold. I did not see the faces of those who hazed me. I know only two of the Sans Soucians personally, and these two slightly. My evidence would, therefore, be too purely circumstantial. I do not wish to give it. I beg to be excused."

Not satisfied, two members of the Board had requested that she state the time and manner of her return to her house. Her quick assurance, "My friends found out where I was and came for me. We were all in the gymnasium at half-past nine, in time for the unmasking," was accepted, not without smiles, by her inquisitors. She was allowed to go. She took with her a memory of two rows of white, despairing girl faces. It hurt her not a little. She could not rejoice in the Sans' downfall, though she knew it to be merited.

At the end of the inquiry the verdict was unanimous for expellment, to go into effect at once. The culprits were given one week to pack and arrange with their families for their return home.

Leslie Cairns had received the major share of blame. Throughout the inquiry she had worn an exasperating air of indifference, which she had doggedly fought to maintain. Not a muscle of her rugged face had moved during the reading of the long letter written by Dulcie Vale to the president. She had laconically admitted the truth of it, coolly correcting one or two erroneous statements Dulcie had made. Afterward, in her room, she had broken down and sobbed bitterly. This no one but herself knew.

The disgraced seventeen left Hamilton for New York on the seventh morning after sentence had been pronounced upon them. They departed early in the morning before the majority of the Wayland Hall girls were up and stirring. Marjorie was glad not to witness their departure. She had not approved of them. Still they were young girls like herself. She experienced a certain pity for their weakness of character. Jerry, however, was openly delighted to be rid of her pet abomination.

With the approach of May Day the Nine Travelers had something pleasant to look forward to. Miss Susanna had sent them invitations to dinner on May Day evening. Very gleefully they planned to deluge the mistress of Hamilton Arms with May baskets. These they intended to leave in one of the two automobiles which they would use. After dinner, Ronny had volunteered to slip away from the party, secure the baskets and place them before the front door. She would lift the knocker, then scurry inside, leaving Jonas, who was to be in the secret, to call Miss Susanna to the door.

When, as Miss Hamilton's guests on May Day evening, they were ushered into the beautiful, mahogany-panelled dining room at Hamilton Arms, a surprise awaited them. The long room, an apartment of state in Brooke Hamilton's day, was a veritable bower of violets. Bouquets of them, surrounded by their own decorative green leaves were in evidence everywhere in the room. They were the double English variety, and their fragrance was as a sweet breath of spring. A scented purple mound of them occupied the center of the dining table. It was topped by a familiar object; a willow, ribbon-trimmed basket. As on the previous May Day evening it was full of violets. Narrow violet satin ribbon depended from the center of the basket to each place, at which set a small replica of the basket Marjorie had left before Miss Susanna's door, just one year ago that evening.

"I knew Miss Susanna would guess who went Maying a year ago this evening!" Jerry exclaimed. "After you had known Marvelous Marjorie a little while the guessing came easy, didn't it?" She turned impulsively to Miss Hamilton.

"Yes; you are quite correct, Jerry," the old lady made quick answer. "One year ago tonight was a very happy occasion for me. Violets were Uncle Brooke's favorite flower. I cannot tell you how strangely I felt at sight of that basket. Jonas came into the library and asked me to go to the front door. He said in his solemn way: 'There's something at the door I would like you to see, Miss Susanna.' He looked so mysterious, I rose at once from my chair and went to the door. I must explain, too, that the first of May was Uncle Brooke's

birthday. When I looked out and saw that basket
of violets, it was like a silent message from him.
Jonas had no more idea than I from whom the
lovely May offering had come. He had heard the
clang of the knocker, but when he opened the door
there was not a soul in sight. The good fairy had
vanished, leaving me a fragrant May Day remembrance."

Marjorie had laughed at first sight of the familiar basket. She was still smiling, rather tremu-
lously, however. The beauty of the decorations,
the fragrance of the violets and the amazing knowledge that she had brought Brooke Hamilton's favorite flower to the doorstep on the anniversary of his
birth, made strong appeal to the fund of sentiment
which lay deep within her, rarely coming to the
surface.

"How came you to remember a crotchety person
like me, child?" Miss Susanna's bright brown eyes
were soft with tenderness. She reached forward
and took both Marjorie's hands in hers.

Thus they stood for an instant, youth and age,
beside the violet-crowned table. The other girls,
lovely in their pale-hued evening frocks, surrounded
the pair with smiling faces.

"I—I don't know," stammered Marjorie. "I—I
thought perhaps you would like it. I couldn't resist
putting it on your doorstep. We were all making

May baskets to hang on one another's doors. I thought of you. I knew you loved flowers, because I had seen you working among them. That's all."

"No, that was only the beginning." Miss Susanna released Marjorie's hands. "It gave me much to think of for many months; in fact until a little girl put aside her own plans to help a poor old lady pick up a basket of spilled chrysanthemums."

Appearing a trifle embarrassed at her own rush of sentiment, Miss Hamilton turned to the others and proceeded briskly to seat her guests at table. While she occupied the place at the head, she gave Marjorie that at the foot. Lifting the little basket at her place to inhale the perfume of the flowers, something dropped therefrom. It struck against the thin water glass at her place with a little clang. Next instant she was exclaiming over a dainty lace pin of purple enameled violets with tiny diamond centers.

"I would advise all of you to do a little exploring." Miss Susanna's voice held a note of suppressed excitement.

Obeying with the zest of girlhood, the others found pretty lace pins of gold and silver, chosen with a view toward suiting the personality of each.

As Marjorie fastened her new possession on the bodice of the violet-tinted crêpe gown, which had been Mah Waeo's gift to her father for her, she had a feeling of living in a fairy tale. Hamilton Arms had always seemed as an enchanted castle to her. She had never expected to penetrate its fastnesses and become an honored guest within its walls.

"Miss Susanna, when did you first guess that it was I who left you a May basket?" she asked, rather curiously. "Lucy and Jerry said you would find me out. I didn't think so."

"It was after Christmas, Marjorie," the old lady replied. "Perhaps it was the bunch of violets on the wreath you girls sent for Uncle Brooke's study that established the connection. I really can't say. It dawned upon me all of a sudden one evening. I spoke of it to Jonas. The old rascal simply said: 'Oh, yes. I have thought so for a long time.' Not a word to me of it had he peeped. It furnished me with pleasant thoughts for so long, I decided that one good turn deserves another. I succeeded in surprising you children tonight, but no one could have been more astonished than I when I gathered in that blessed violet basket last May Day night."

CHAPTER XXVII

CONCLUSION

"And tomorrow is another day; the great day!" Leila Harper sat with clasped hands behind her head, fondly viewing her chums.

The Nine Travelers had gathered in her room for a last intimate talk. Tomorrow would be Commencement. Directly after the exercises were over the nine had agreed to meet for a last celebration at Baretti's. Evening of that day would see them all going their appointed ways.

"I can't make it seem true that you girls won't be back here next year," Marjorie said dolefully, setting down her lemonade glass with a despondent thump, a half-eaten maccaroon poised in mid-air.

"Eat your sweet cake child and don't weep," consoled Leila. While she was trying hard to look sad, there was a peculiar gleam in her blue eyes. As yet Marjorie had failed to catch it.

"Nothing will seem the same," grumbled Jerry. "With you four good scouts lifted out of college garden there will be an awful vacancy." Jerry fixed almost mournful eyes on Helen. "Why couldn't you girls have entered a year later or else we a year earlier?" she asked retrospectively.

"Cheer up, Jeremiah. The worst is yet to come." Vera patted Jerry on the back. Standing behind Jerry's chair she cast an odd glance at Leila. Leila passed it on to Helen, who in turn telegraphed some mute message to Katherine Langly.

"I can't see it," Jerry said, her round face unusually sober. "It is hard enough now to have to lose four good pals at one swoop. I sha'n't feel any worse at the last minute tomorrow than I do tonight. I have an actual case of the blues this evening which even lemonade and cakes won't dispel."

"Let us not talk about it," advised Veronica. "Every time the subject comes up we all grow solemn."

"I'm worse off than the rest of you," complained Muriel. "I am torn between two partings. I can't bear to think of losing good old Moretense."

"While we are on the subject of partings," began Leila, ostentatiously clearing her throat, "I regret that I shall have to say something which can but add to your sorrow. I—that is——" She looked at Vera and burst into laughter which carried a distinctly happy note.

"What ails you, Leila Greatheart?" Marjorie focussed her attention on the Irish girl's mirthful face. "I am just beginning to see that something unusual is on foot. "The idea of parading mysteries before us at the very last minute of your journey through the country of college!"

" 'Tis a beautiful country, that." Leila spoke purposely, with a faint brogue. "And did you say it was my last minute there? Suppose it was not? What? As our departed bogie, Miss Cairns, used to say."

"Do you know what you are talking about?" inquired Jerry. "I hope you do. I haven't caught the drift of your remarks—yet."

"Do you tell her then, Midget." Leila fell suddenly silent, her Cheshire cat grin ornamenting her features.

"Oh, let Helen tell it. She knows." Vera beamed on Helen, who passed the task, whatever it might be, on to Katherine. She declined, throwing it back to Leila.

"What is this bad news that none of you will take upon yourselves to tell us?" Lucy's green eyes sought Katherine's in mock reproach.

"I have it." Leila held up a hand. Now; altogether! We are going to——" she nodded encouragement to Kathie, Vera and Helen.

"We are going to stay!" shouted four voices in concert.

"Stay where? What do——" Jerry stopped

abruptly. Her face relaxed of a sudden into one
of her wide smiles. She rose and began hugging
Helen, shouting: "You don't mean it? Honestly?"

The rest of the Lookouts were going through
similar demonstrations of joy. For a moment or
two everyone talked and laughed at once. Gradually the first noisy reception of the news subsided
and Leila could be heard:

"It's like this, children," she said. "Vera wants
to specialize in Greek. I am still keen on physics
and psychology. Helen wants to make a new and
more comprehensive study of literature, and Kathie
is going to teach English. Miss Fernald is leaving
and Kathie is to have her place. We've had all we
could do to keep it from you. Vera and I might
better be here next year than at home. We'd have
not much to do there. We are anxious to help
make the dream of the dormitory come true."

"It is too beautiful for anything!" was Marjorie's childish but heartfelt rejoicing. "With you
four to help us next year we shall accomplish wonders. Oh, I shall love being a senior!"

What Marjorie's senior year at Hamilton
brought her will be told in "MARJORIE DEAN,
COLLEGE SENIOR."

THE END

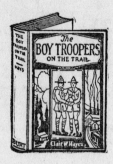

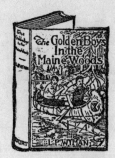